CK

BRING OUT YOUR DEAD

By the same author
Across the Water
Candles and Dark Night
Head of the Corner
Last Dance with You

BRING OUT YOUR DEAD

Grace Ingoldby

PETER OWEN
LONDON AND CHESTER SPRINGS

PETER OWEN PUBLISHERS
73 Kenway Road, London SW5 ORE
Peter Owen books are distributed in the USA by Dufour Editions Inc.,
Chester Springs, PA 19425-0007

First published in Great Britain 1998
ISBN 0 7206 1061 3

A catalogue record for this book is available from the British Library

Printed and made in Great Britain by Hillman Printers (Frome) Ltd

TALNET	
Morley Books	21.3.00
F	£14.99

With thanks to
Edward Abelson and Keiran Pheland,
without whom . . .

For those in peril on the sea

I am but mad north-north-west; when the wind is southerly, I know a hawk from a handsaw.

Hamlet

Part 1

ABOVE it all, where the third-floor windows look out on to parkland that has been sculpted, sloped, rounded and curved, that has had its very nap smoothed to ease the eye, Dr Michael Swan is sitting for his portrait. Blessed with the regular features favoured by knitting patterns, with hair that, luxuriant and bouncy, deep black and curly, looks at its best two days after a wash, Dr Swan is – and knows he is – attractive.

Resplendent this fine September morning in a white, tan-enhancing, shoulder-buttoned clinical coat that is softly starched and can't be itchy, he seems to have a problem sitting still.

'A little to the right, doctor? That's it . . . lovely jubbly.'

The painter beams at Swan, who beams back at the painter; this commission is important to them both. Throughout the summer of 1997 fax machines have clicked and whistled and, though the subject is now arranged to the artist's satisfaction, all will come to nothing if the man can't hold his pose.

Portraits of chief medical officers of PAIN, the Pauper Asylum and Institute for Neurotics, are part of a grand tradition dating from 1862 and hanging, curiously high up, around its marble-tiled and barrel-vaulted entrance hall.

Josephine Foxley, 1852–60, in the crispest of bonnets and an expanse of purplish-brown bosom like a moor. Her portrait, painted in the fourteenth-century pose of a carved *Virgin con Niest* is, like many lessons from the past, difficult to decipher now. Her upraised hand holds a miniature replica of the Whirling Chair invented by her grandfather on the premise that shaking things up helped to settle things down, but who or what sits on her knee may only be guessed at; the painting has been neglected, and detail, like an escaped prisoner, is lost against the moor.

Jungians and Freudians, cranioscopists, phrenologists, physiognomists, forced through the accident of hanging to look each other in the eye. The stern, the serene and the simply sexy, Ivan Clampit, Hilary Shadbolt, Simon Pentecost. As the painter looks from the sitter to his palate to his picture, what he sees is not hair follicles nourished by conditioner but a narrowing around the eyes and a pinched look to the usually full lips of the mouth. The face has altered since the summer, but one does not ask a doctor how he is feeling. What was once cavalier and confident now looks not crushed exactly but as if it had been crammed into the wrong-sized envelope.

The artist, Hedley Branscome Baker, had faxed Swan; Swan had faxed artist. Though neither had any wish to transcend the inherent substantiality of oils, dissension pivoted on whether the portrait should be head and shoulders or full length. The result of these extended negotiations is a seated pose enhanced by a collection of objects placed on a low table in the foreground. Swan's asthma inhaler (the personal struggle with the bronchi must not go unsung), a computer mouse with mouse mat and a bound copy of Swan's paper on 'Psychic Numbing'. A formal distance rather than a bedside manner is to be evoked; the artist at pains to capture all that epitomizes the dignity of the sitter and simultaneously distils the essence of the era over which he has prevailed. The continuity of mental health care – that grand history – is illustrated by a pestle and mortar in one hand and a primed syringe in the other. What at this stage are simply sketches in the background will represent the hands of many ex-inmates waving good-bye as they return, as they must do in the stringent nineties, to the wild.

'And one of those brain slices,' the artist requests, as if he is addressing Doreen Brande, the doyenne of PAIN's canteen.

The chosen slice is an enlarged computer-coloured photograph mounted against black. Rose madder pinks and cadmium yellows, ultramarine and viridian: psyche-delic colours illustrating the occipital lobe, parietal lobe, cerebrum and cerebellum. The medulla that connects the brain to the spinal cord is a mass of scorching fuchsia, the whole as phosphorescent and as surprisingly beautiful as oil dripped in a muddy puddle. Only the final triumph of science over the church is missing, the artist's suggestion that Swan's feet rest upon a recumbent chaplain proving ultimately too delicate to organize.

Sustained by an image of the final product the painter stabs at the canvas, repeating to himself the handy mantra that nothing is achieved without proper fear. The commis-sion is due to be hung in December and finding a place to squeeze it into the gallery has been truly vexing. The obvi-ous choice of hanging Swan chronologically, next to his immediate predecessor Hubert Bottril – a pallid watercolour that looks as if it were painted by his wife – was rejected on the premise that disgrace can be contagious and it is deemed more sensitive to tuck it between Ivan Clampit, spoon-faced but successful, and Robert Wilder, 1963–7, a brilliant career cut short by a mysterious seaside car accident. Wilder, the only chief medical officer to embrace photography, will provide a splendid foil to this oil commission. There is something of Fellini in Wilder's choice of late sixties photo-montage: the sitter is shown cross-legged and holding a daisy on the grass tennis-court, the wire frame of which is hung randomly with lifebelts. Beyond this we see the unmistakable façade of PAIN, the towering central blocks of Hilversum, Luxembourg, Roma and Finisterre; half Italianate, half classical and presently half empty.

'We're losing your neck, doctor. Just relax your shoulders if you can.'

Only delete, thinks Dr Michael Swan this morning. No 'P' for pending in this department, no asterisks, no question marks. Is it possible that until this moment he has never truly looked at his colleagues or is it that, shoved into close proximity with them now, sitting in the foyer of his newly refurbished department, forced to watch them come and go and be, that they have finally, bloodily, impinged?

Paula, loyal secretary. Swan objected to the frequency with which she blew her nose. Keeping his pose meant looking towards the photo cube prominently displayed upon her desk, showing a picture of a large bald baby in a reclining car seat. Once or twice he had felt himself floating into that picture, driven along in that car and before he could utter the word 'Stop!' he was off to the supermarket with its parents. Paula's sister and her brother-in-law, they were all there, strolling down the aisles in search of oven chips, the baby lolling in the trolley, its Aunt Paula pecking at her nose.

'I think we're going to have to let you go,' Swan muses as his colleague Dr Beaker arrives late, engine oil on his anorak, bulging briefcase softly bumping against fat corduroy legs. Dr Beaker, sharing a joke with Dr Orchid Witty, light falling on Orchid's bobbed blonde hair.

'I think we're going to have to knock you on the head.'
'Chin up, doctor, but don't smile.'
Precious little chance of that.

Full lips slightly pinched this morning and on such close inspection a punch-drunk, wary look about the eyes. As Hedley looks at Dr Swan, what he sees are the eyes of Jocelyn Jocelyn, 1897–1919. Jocelyn, who single-handedly dragged PAIN across the border into the twentieth century, whose features speak of the responsibilities – at its peak the asylum boasted three thousand inmates and a pack of hounds – that must bear heavily even upon the broadest back. It was Jocelyn who forbore when the asylum was requisitioned as a hospital during the Great War, and even a cursory glance at his portrait shows that the esteemed phrenologist gained no comfort whatsoever from the display of measuring equipment so carefully arranged before him in enamelled kidney bowls. The fingers that felt so many bumps are tightly knotted, the shoulders, like Swan's shoulders, hunched. The cause of all this tension lies greenly in the background of the painting, the fernery that Jocelyn established in the Wet Weather Room, the fernery on which he lavished such a large proportion of his time. For no sooner had Jocelyn achieved the appropriate level of humidity for ferns, melancholics moving among the fronds with mist sprays harnessed to their shoulders, than much of the collection was devastated by an influx of unsteady amputees.

September sunlight floods the foyer that, facing south, is the most coveted of the four asylum blocks. Sunlight that fails to take the edge off Swan's anxiety and he knows –

because understandably he loves himself, because, understandably, he analyses himself relentlessly – that he is
undergoing something, struggling through a cloud of
something; that he is experiencing a blip. Nine weeks now
since his mother died while packing up the family
home . . . as Swan sits so the blip whips its tail into its
mouth and, sitting as he must in this silence, he cranes
forward towards the end of the blip while pondering
simultaneously the beginning.

He was due to see his mother, but he was later than he
should have been because he had been with Orchid Witty,
in the days when being with Orchid Witty was a pleasure
not a pain. He had let himself into the house and found his
mother sprawled on the terrace of blue lias, one hand
clutching a piece of string. The pose, her pose, an old lady
in a cardigan spread across the stones, was even at the time
– particularly at the time – a double take. He had felt as if
he'd seen it before, then realized he *had* seen it before,
illustrated in a magazine. Perfect to the very last detail,
false teeth and liver spots, except of course for the string.
One shoe was off, as one shoe always was, and there was
something else missing. What was it? It was the bleeper
that was missing, the bleepers sons bought for their
mothers, the bleepers that kept mothers ticking, allowing
them to summon help after falling. He had backed in
through the french windows, retreated to the sitting-room
and tried to find something to cover her with. For some
reason – it was hellish to recall it now – he had lit on the
loose cover of the sofa, crouching beside it, tearing at its
hooks and eyes; then, realizing that this was absolutely
silly, grabbing the cushions and laying them on her, one
upon her abdomen where her blue blouse had come loose
from her skirt and revealed her slippery petticoat, one over
her face. He had whipped that one off sharpish, it looked

as if he had tried to suffocate her . . . Then he had gone back in again, unplugged the phone and taken it into the dining-room to call his sister Margaret. The string in his mother's hand, how it tugged him; she had always insisted they save string. And that had been the first thing he had said to his wife, Julia:

'Presumably, when your mother's dead, you're permitted to waste string?'

'You're frowning, doctor. Just relax your brow.'

The doctor adjusted his gaze, focused on the tree-pipit blue of the skirting-board. All his own efforts (well, with a bit of help from Orchid); together they had turned the department around from clinical/clerical to something resembling the cool serenity of a dappled glade. Green. He and Orchid had spent an afternoon (well, part of one) choosing the colours, juxtaposing them, rejecting some and toying with others, setting juniper against sap, emerald against olive. And that was the point, he thought, not able to stop himself altering his pose and getting ticked off again, at which they should have disposed of the anachronism, the department's mobile tank of fish.

'Your father's on the line, doctor. Shall I say to call back later?'

Swan took the phone call in his room.

'Dad. Hello. How's it going?'

'How do you think it's going?'

Swan stood with the receiver, looking out of his window, parting the – again brand new – vertical linen blinds, but the view that had been landscaped to soothe him failed. What caught his eye was the distant glint of water in the swimming pool, dug out by inmates during the troubled reign of his predecessor, Hubert Bottril. Foolhardy to situate the pool so close to the boundary wall, to arm inmates with heavy forks and spades . . . Somebody, Swan couldn't remember who, some inmate had escaped.

When Swan had told his father to ring at any time he hadn't meant it. Letters he could have coped with, letters he could have shoved aside.

'I thought you were going to drop me a line, Dad.'

'On writing paper that's headed with a ball of wool and —'

'You're exaggerating.'

'Believe me, I am not.'

'Look, once your leg —'

'Bugger my leg, Michael!'

Swan's father had recently moved – been moved – to a nursing home, a painful transition that had been exacerbated when he had tripped over a chair-lift during a fire-drill in his second week.

'I'm only saying —'

'It's not my leg that worries me, it's . . . I'm —'

His father sounded breathless. All the male Swans were asthmatic. Michael remembered his mother saying how much she was looking forward to single beds in the new house, how sick and tired she was of waking to find the plastic lid of her husband's inhaler embedded in her thigh.

'Take it easy, Dad.'

'Nothing to do but sit all day waggling my thumbs. I used to garden —'

'Once your leg —'

'Do you know I haven't been outside for seven days, Michael.'

'The weather's been awful.'

'You don't know how lucky you are.'

Swan senior didn't know how lucky he was; somewhere decent . . .

'How are the deer?' Swan asked. Bloody lucky to be in a nursing home that was attractively landscaped, deer roaming free among the oak trees, Zimmers fringing the ornamental pond.

'I don't see any bloody deer. She's moved me, Mrs Eversley. I look out on to a bit of motorway planting, I look out on to a bloody bund!'

'I can't talk for too long, Dad.'

His father snorted.

'I think you're . . . I know its difficult —'

'You don't know!'

'But there's no point . . . you're getting things out of perspective.'

'That's what you say to your patients, I suppose?'

'Once your leg —'

'Did you know that there isn't even any carpet upstairs, Michael? Did you know that? And I know why. I know why! I've got the book, you see. Now that surprised you, didn't it?'

'What book?'

'*The* book. *The* book, Michael. Hang on. Hang on. They're saving money, that's the long and short of it. Just let me quote. Just you listen to this. Just —'

'Dad —'

His father lowered his voice. '"Old people do not lift their feet when walking . . . because their muscles get weak with age and . . . carpets get quickly worn out. A shuffling gait . . ."' – his voice rose – '"A shuffling gait, plus walking frames and wheelchairs . . ."'

His father started wheezing.

'"The journey . . . to the bedside commode . . . is much . . . shortened . . . than that to the toilet . . ."' – between you and your sister you've managed to put me in a place where they can't even write bloody English! – "Most residents . . ." I'm quoting now . . .'

Swan turned from the window just in time to catch sight of Dr Beaker wheeling the fish tank into his office.

'Can you hold a minute, Dad?'

'Don't bother about me!'

Laying the receiver upon the desk Swan took his diary and turning to the back added a single stroke to a column of identical marks beneath the heading 'Beaker/Fish'. Closing the book, he looked through the glass into the foyer. Oh great, he said to himself. Brilliant. Through the window he could see the artist in conversation with Orchid. How long had this been going on? And Swan could tell by the way she handed him a paper cup of water that she too was keen. Well, so be it. It was over anyway and his wife Julia still wouldn't talk to him. You don't get sex when you're going through a blip.

'Julia has taken up piano,' he told his father. 'Very keen.'

'Lucky to have music.'

'Yes, we're very lucky.' Swan agrees.

'Dr Swan? I shouldn't really divulge. It's embarrassing,' Dee says to her friend Maisie as they circle the square of the Airing Court after their lunch.

Clouds blow briskly in the rectangle of sky they see above them, clouds that are businesslike, on their way to somewhere else. Maisie clings to Dee's elbow, her free hand tapping her walking stick against the asphalt. Shuffling along, her stumpy legs shoved into a pair of cut-off wellingtons, her body curved backwards, her head tilted upwards, eyes monitoring the roof-tops of the four huge blocks that surround them. Dee gets a thrill out of frightening Maisie. She has told her there is a sniper on the roof.

'"Do stay, Dee," he says. Well, "No debts there," I said to him. "I'm not going to say sorry, Michael, because sorry I am not." Threw himself at me during his first week. Oh well, you know, private sessions in his room, that sort of thing. I said, "Look, dear, let's face it, you're talking to someone who could have had a fling with Gorbachov." That was it, he said I made him laugh. Laugh? As if that was what he was put here for. But very rough, oh yes. I told him, "I shall be writing to the Independent Complaints Committee about this." That scares them, Maisie, mark my words. And I did. I'm as good as my word. I wrote, "Dear MIND, just get this man not simply off my back but struck off!" No response, not a dicky bird. "Lists," I wrote. "I can give you lists, places, times and seasons." But no. It's very John le Carré, MIND. Dead letter-boxes, Moscow parks, those discouraging flats.'

Dee is on splendid form this afternoon. A good week, this week, her first week working in the laundry with Eddie. The orange tabard they all wear, the letters PAIN stamped front and back, sits neatly across her shoulders and is done up properly on both sides. When Dee is on form she always tucks herself in neatly, polishes her small court shoes. If Maisie can't see the sniper then she is keeping quiet about it. Dee will say she isn't looking hard enough; no, if she can't see the sniper then it is probably her fault. Dee is full of premonitions and dark purple foreboding. She says she hasn't got her dog with her today because of the atmosphere; this morning she told Eddie in the laundry that they would probably be gassed. 'Gas that doesn't smell like gas, Eddie.' Does Dee really believe it? She believes Eddie is the one for her; that is more to the point. Eddie is so fine looking. His hair is receding, which makes him look intelligent – he is intelligent – and she likes that. Vague, distinctly non-committal, 'Abstracted, if you ask me, Maisie, very keen on sex.' Dee is keen, too, but it is difficult to know quite how to go about it, how to bring up the subject first thing on a working morning; better to begin with gas. 'They'll pipe it up through the ventilation system and we won't know what's hit us because we'll be asleep.'

Dee talks of gas as if she would relish the attention. Though older than Eddie her made-up face is childishly wistful, a wide forehead covered with a thick brown fringe. For years her hair has been cut by the same nurse. Dee is used to the result.

The laundry where they are set to work is an elegant room running along the lower floor of Luxembourg and opposite the abandoned block of Finisterre. It is from here that Dee's idea of gas originates. Something strange and obviously secret is going on at the back of Finisterre. The top of a massive crane can be seen and heard quite clearly from the Airing Court. The laundry is high ceilinged, well proportioned, with three long barred windows that look out over the court. Sparsely furnished, it has drying racks against its inside wall, a set of benches and two long scrubbed tables. On the corner of one sits the sewing machine where Dee is meant to work. Eddie empties out a canvas sack of laundry and sorts the smelly contents into a pile. Beyond the window another inmate, William Carter, – 'Barely out of short trousers,' Dee said to Maisie – passes through the court, wheeling his cleaning trolley. Dee taps the window.

'Won't you come in, William?'

'Later,' he shouts.

'Boring,' says Dee. 'Eddie?'

'What?'

'I don't know what you see in him.'

'In whom?'

'In William. William never understands. I said to Maisie, "He doesn't understand, you know, how can he comprehend? He's not a plateau dweller like us, Maisie, how can William understand? He's a blow-in, darling," I said to her, "and it isn't safe or sensible to be friends with him." You know what you're like, Eddie, we don't want you getting hurt. I'm not dictating to you in any way. Believe me, I know best. In, out and never keep in touch with anybody. Not worth it in the long run, wouldn't you say so, Eddie, dear? Not that he isn't appealing in a country sort of way, all long legs and hayricks, but it takes more than that in my book to add up to fresh air. I told him to get out quickly before he's turfed into the lime-pit with the rest of us, carted off like plague victims who can't appreciate the finer points of life.'

Dee glances at the sewing machine. She isn't ready for it yet. Instead she potters about the large room, shutting cupboard doors that Eddie would prefer left open, drumming her small hands along the bars of the drying racks.

'Look at that, Eddie. Eddie, look!' She indicates the moving neck of the crane, quite visible from the windows. 'We all know what's dangling from that, don't we, Eddie? That's the soft-toy portacabin. And no one had the chance to say goodbye. Classrooms lifted off without so much as a by-your-leave. Is nothing sacred, Eddie? Eddie? Don't you care? And who's to say there's not a sniper on the roof?' Sniper. It was at that point that she decided to save the word for Maisie. It had such a nice serrated edge. 'Absolutely no point giving up smoking. Increase the intake, that's what I think. Not going to die of lung cancer, are we, if we're going to be gassed?'

Eddie has made a pile of drill trousers, of blue and white

striped work shirts. He checks each one for lost buttons and torn pockets as he sorts the clothes. Anything in need of mending he places to one side for Dee.

'Hubert wouldn't have let this happen,' Dee says. Dropping the name of their Number One Man on to the stone floor and watching with some satisfaction as it bounces towards Eddie at the far end of the room.

'What happen?'

'"No angel might stub its toe." Eddie, do you remember that?'

'Yes,' says Eddie, standing up to ease his back. 'It was "No angel . . . no one of you . . ."'

'It had a wonky frame and no glass on it. You remember, Eddie. It hung near the fish tank, just as you go in the door.'

'He toasted it when he was drinking.'

'No, Eddie. Don't say that.'

'It was, "No angel . . ."' Eddie tries to recreate the quote. '"No angel . . . none of you . . ."'

Where quotations are concerned Eddie feels obliged to get them absolutely right. Precision is a habit of his that Dee finds profoundly irritating. Now that she has got his attention she really wants to move on quickly to what really matters: the two of them and sex.

'Forget it, Eddie.'

'"No angel . . ."'

'It doesn't matter, Eddie. Just forget it. I wish I hadn't brought it up.'

Eddie nibbles at his nails. '"No angel . . ."'

'Shut up,' says Dee. 'Shut up.'

But Eddie won't shut up. Once he has begun there is no stopping him, tripping on the words, losing confidence, going back to the beginning again, again. The motto that hung in the psychiatry department when Hubert Bottril was chief MO. It hung over the fish tank . . .

'Shut up!' Dee shouts. 'Shut up!'

It's a bugger, her first morning, and it's all going so wrong. 'Shut up!' she says, getting up from her chair and knocking it sideways on to the floor in agitation, kicking at the piles of shirts and trousers round Eddie, kicking out at him.

'Knock it off,' says Warren, a young male nurse who has heard the racket.

'Knock it off,' says Dee.

'I said, shut it, Dorothy.'

'Dorothy' is humiliating and horrid, unfair; she can't stand up against it, a jet of freezing water that paradoxically makes her feel clammy and hot. Dorothy, the name written on the file her father had; Dorothy, squashed, shoved into a drawer.

Humiliated, hot, Dee returns to her sewing machine. Warren watches from the door. Her armpits are prickling with embarrassment, there is sweat between her breasts and on her forehead. She rights her chair and picks her handbag off the floor and clutches it to her, sitting with her arms folded around it. Eddie, too, is flustered. He runs his hands round and round and round the next canvas sack of washing. Yet it is Dee who is first to recover. Cooling fast she empties the contents of her handbag on to the floor.

'You'll go back to the ward, so knock it off!' warns Warren.

She knows he can't be bothered to do that. Lazy, layabout boy, stripling. Dee takes her time with the handbag, stooping down and picking up each object individually. As she does this, so she regains her old composure, so that by the time she has got it all back in the bag again she is Dee again.

'Tell me,' she says to Warren in a cool voice, 'why is it

that you, so beautiful and so young, speak in such a horrid cut-off manner. "Knock it off!"' she mimics. '"Knock it off and shut it." All the lovely limpid things you could say but you feel you can't, I suppose. You haven't got the confidence – or did no one ever teach you how to address persons of a different class? You feel you must speak like that, do you, speak like that to us? If I may say so, Warren, it's all deeply unattractive. "Knock it off!"' she mimics. '"Knock it off, leave it out!"' she says in a singsong voice. '"Shut it . . ."'

There is another world but this one. Eddie rubs his hand over his eyes. Warren remains in the doorway. Eddie pulls the drying racks out from the wall, their castors grating on the metal track. He will be all right once he is working again: there is another world but this one. So he drags the second canvas sack into the corner and turns his back on Dee and Warren, emptying out a pile of socks.

'Orchid wants to take me out in the car, you know,' Dee says. 'I told her, "I'm not usually sick in cars, Orchid, but I know I should be profoundly sick in yours."'

Warren has left the doorway. Both of them notice but neither remark on it. Eddie puts the first load in the washing-machine. Dee, who hasn't made one stitch so far this morning, pushes her chair back from the table and fishes in her handbag for a cigarette.

'"Don't trill your little tray of tablets around me," I told her. "You obviously don't know me. When my head hits the pillow, dear, I'm off."'

When Eddie's head hits the pillow, William Carter wakes him. Eddie is the rock that William lives on, shelters under. The only thing safer than Eddie is death. If Eddie ducks his head beneath the blankets William will feel for his hand.

On the dormitory in Luxembourg Eddie and William

have pushed their beds together to escape the pools of orange light that cut through any curtain, the all-day, all-night hiss – which when you tune in to it becomes a zing – of the newly erected sodium lights. William dreams and dozes, cannot sleep, is chronically insomniac. His young face is discoloured by dark patches of skin. Sleep! He would sleep in a halved pipe if he could get his hands on one, in a swaddling cot with edges high enough to reassure. A curve of comfort is what William Carter craves, not the straightened utility of a narrow, single bed. Sleep! For Eddie it is a hole that he must skirt around. Lying next to the restless William, Eddie's hands are clenched. William is a burden Eddie carries; only when he hears the even sound of sleepy breathing from the next bed can Eddie go, where he longs to go, alone.

Sleep stands in Eddie's path but with practice he can slip right by it to recall a tiredness of a different kind. His mind's eye looks to the coastal map of Nova Scotia, tracing the soft-edged crescent of a bay. Finding it he lies his body the full length of it. Here is tiredness of another sort. Tiredness that will soothe and reassure him, the sweet, uncomplicated tiredness of child-sleep, bare arms stretched above the head. Tiredness as soft as padded satin, the tiredness of a seaside day.

Careful, easy, every spot is tender, memory is the ultimate gum disease. Upon the path now, Eddie taps an arc around him to pick his way towards the precious, to slip through the boulders that strew the way into the past and find 'Once upon a time . . .' and, as his eyes droop, 'Long ago and far away . . .'

A pebbly beach, full at the height of the day but from four thirty onwards, you could bank on it, the crowds beginning to disperse. Other families pack up and go, then you could take your pick and have the spot you wanted all along. By six the shouts of all the other children, the crying of stumbling babies, was quite gone, replaced by the squalling of the gulls that had been there in the background all the time. The new tide licking at the bits of picnic debris, lifting the lost spade, sinking the forgotten hat. Then there was one last swim. Cold now with the sun on the wane, but you got through it anyway, the last swim, followed by the last looks . . . careful, easy, there are words that are difficult to say . . . And the family, his family, a family lulled by a day by the water. Easy steps back along the empty strand. Cold after the last swim, you wore your jumper; the picnic bags were light now, the flasks empty, but the towels were heavier than they had been, salt-logged and water-logged. Easy silence descending as they trouped along. Over the uneven stones, past the wooden decking where the divers gathered now with their equipment. Safe to think about that. Weights and gas bottles on the wooden decking, away from the waves now but not from the sound of sea, which comes all the way home with you, which turns you gently in your bed. Up past the coastguard cottages and the rusty anchors where, earlier that day, a loud group had collected money for the lifeboat. That sweet tiredness, the water that turns you . . .

Eddie lays his hands behind his head, unaware that there are others – eyes closed, walking – on Hilversum, on Roma and even here on Luxembourg all attempting the same thing. If William will only leave him be now, if William will only let him lie.

Eddie walks the track past the divers, past the coastguard cottages, walks it as others around him, as others before him, now walk about the houses, gardens, streets, parks they knew beyond these walls. Make cups of tea, take mugs off hooks, open and close familiar cupboards. A path carved through the boulders, a serious game, and the skilled, like divers, walking backwards of an evening, backwards into the water in their flippers, schooled in this high art. Time to dream is limited, is precious. They schooled themselves so they too could fall backwards, could plunge directly, deeply, safely, in.

So the incarcerated wander in their imaginations, hop on buses, cross the bridge, push the door that jams in clammy weather. Get change from purses, retouch their make-up in the powder rooms of pubs. This is the art of survival, choosing the right path, a clear run, a moonlit night to do it in. Inmates travel in their heads along well-beaten tracks, antennae stretched – the effort is never over – desperate for the smallest added token, for the gift that selective memory might throw up. The gift of one more thing that they can bear to contemplate, another signpost that points directly to what it felt like then. The wrapper from a Tizer bottle, blown and whitened in the hedge; the experienced, the talented may find this, may feel with shaking fingers the lines of glue still there to touch along the label's back. The thesaurus on the shelf, the dictionary that contains somewhere, if you could just get your hands on it, the word that helps to bring it back. The word that describes exactly the sensation that with supreme effort you may remember and thus feel, enjoy, again. English words in English dictionaries that describe the things that English speakers feel. The desperate striving towards improved retrieval of what is bearable, to spot the label, to feel the lines of glue. Improvement beyond the point you thought improvement might take you, mind walking through the boulders, further out and deeper in. This is the gold in the mine that is still working and you have to keep on trying, to keep on digging, you can't let the water in.

Eddie sleeps, William wakes him. William dozes and

Eddie lies awake. William takes solace from religion. When Eddie complains, William likens his friend to Jesus, the son of God, poking the ribs of the apostles in the Garden of Gethsemane; he is surprised when Eddie says this doesn't help. And sometimes in the darkness of the early morning Eddie thinks he hears things; the clang of the Death Bell, the doyng, doyng, doyng, the clang like a sea bell in a Northern ocean . . .

'Take me out in the car and dump me somewhere,' Dee says, clicking her lighter and licking her finger to place it for just a moment in the flame.

Night, thinks Eddie, gazing at the stubborn brute of a clock, willing it to read more than ten past nine.

Dee sleeps very soundly, thank you, rising early to start smoking. She is as committed to tobacco as William is committed to the virgin birth. When Dee smokes she puts the whole top half of her body into it, if not her bottom and both legs. She cups her left hand under her right elbow, flourishing the cigarette, using it as a punctuation aid.

'In any case we'll probably' – flourish – 'be gassed.'

Dee never lets a cigarette die away in an ashtray. She smokes it to the tip then throws it on the floor and grinds it out.

There is another world but this one. Eddie has read about it in a book. '"To dwellers in a wood . . ."' He has got it, the first paragraph, by heart. '"To dwellers in a wood almost every species of tree has its voice as well as its features. Only what is entirely lost demands to be endlessly named . . ."' No, that comes from somewhere else.

Dee smokes. Eddie concentrates, rubbing and rubbing at his face, and gathers in his arms the clothes that need some mending, walking over to Dee and dumping them in a pile around her feet. The sparse furnishing of the laundry is beautiful to Eddie. The creamy-white of those scrubbed tables, the drying racks and benches, all of it brings peace to his eye, monastic peace. Eddie stands for a moment, fingers in his mouth, looking out of the windows into the Airing Court. Concentrating hard he can make it down the page that his brain has memorized. A holly whistles, beech trees rustle, he hears them, sees them . . .

'La, la, la, la, la, la, la!' Dee has started sewing, accompanying herself by singing up and down the scale. The washing-machine, a Nubrite Industrial circa 1974, shudders to a halt between soak and spin. Eddie slaps it and it starts again with a whirr, a judder and a cloud of steam. As it spins a pool of water seeps out from underneath it, darkening the floor. On the wall the Year at a Glance Calendar 1996 curls with condensation, only the shortest day marked in.

'La, la, la — whoopsie-daisy, Christ!' Dee has jammed the sewing machine. She hits the pedal with her foot, the machine labours.

'Eddie, help. Eddie? It's sticking!'

Eddie mops the floor beneath the rusting skirts of the Nubrite. '"On a cold and starry Christmas within living memory . . ."' This line is two-thirds down the page. '"Cold and starry".' Since the erection of the gigantic outside lights they don't see stars in PAIN. Gone are the days when you could get out of bed and look out into the darkness, crane your head up and think that those stars are the same stars . . .

'Please, Eddie!'

'I've had a hard day,' Dee says when he goes down at last to sort out her sewing machine. She slides the Singer across to the side of the table, then tucks in next to Eddie on the bench. 'A very hard day, Eddie.'

The bobbin is completely clogged with thread. He clears it with a tiny screwdriver.

'Sweet,' Dee says of the screwdriver. 'Like a little finger, Eddie, a baby finger,' she says, placing her hand upon his arm. She watches him as he re-threads the machine for her. The line of cotton drawn from the reel, along the top, through an eyelet, down. Around a cog, back through another eyelet and then . . . down. Behind a clip, into the needle, a path she knows, a path that calms her.

'There,' says Eddie, shifting off the bench. Dee grabs at the Velcro strap that dangles from the side of his tabard, pulling him towards her with surprising force.

'Tell me I'm all right, darling,' she says.

'You're fine.'

Dee's outburst with Warren goes unrecorded. Three months into the job and Warren is too disenchanted to pass anything on. This afternoon he works a shift with Mr Dobie. Mr Dobie struts the square with his hands clasped behind his back. Warren lolls against the wall. Dobie works hard at this strutting, at assuming the pose of someone who has not been irrevocably diminished by the new-issue safari jackets the male attendants are now forced to wear. Epaulets are little compensation for the loss of the quasi-military blouson that Dobie had felt so at home in. The blouson that not simply contained his stomach but lent it authority. Stunted and foreshortened by the present style – the tails of the unlined jacket drape limply over his bottom – Dobie struggles against the feeling that he is inappropriately attired; dressed for a stroll about the national heritage, for a Boxing Day lunch, for retirement. 'Holiday clothes,' he says disparagingly to his wife.

Mr Dobie comes from part of the country that does not

believe in holidays. In his home town you got a good kicking if you crossed your legs the wrong way round. So it is that Dobie makes much of the two-way radio clipped to the sagging serge of his pocket, marching rather than walking about the court; turning his cold eye now to the weather, now to the gable clock, now to his colleague Warren slumped against the wall. Now to the polish on his shoes, now to the octagonal water-tower, now to the huge and ancient, worrisome being that was Miller, on whom it paid to keep an eye. Dressed in old suit trousers, greasy fez and a ragged shirt, the remains of a million meals encrusted to his tabard, Miller stands apart from the other inmates in his favourite place, in the centre of the Airing Court, next to the single walnut tree.

'On the head, Dobie!'

With the dignity due to his position Mr Dobie steps around the drinks can kicked in his direction. Inmates Ridout, Ruck and Fatty Barrett are having a makeshift game of football. Verne, of the neck brace, moves awkwardly in a goal mouth made from two tabards lain upon the ground. Verne can't move fast enough to save anything, which is precisely why he is there. The skittering noise of the drinks can is getting on Dobie's nerves, but he overcomes it, as he is paid to. If there is a banging and a crashing, if a bloody great crane can be seen by all, then Mr Dobie will not let himself rise to it. What crashes and what bangs is no concern of theirs. If now and then the sound of an invisible builder can be heard whistling 'Blue Moon', where the sound comes from and what it signifies is not for them to know.

Dee is strolling arm in arm with Maisie. 'If I had to choose,' she says, 'I think it would have to be Derek Jacobi. So gentle. So considerate. I remember saying at the time, wagging my finger at him, "Derek," I said, "you are spoiling me!" A dear man,' she says loudly for Eddie's benefit, flashing him a smile.

If Eddie notices he doesn't show it. He sits on a bench with William Carter and, like boys who appear to play together but are in fact content to play apart, the two follow their own fancies that afternoon. Eddie has his book beside him, opening it and then closing it, mouthing what he can remember of the words. William is preoccupied with grease-proof paper, busying himself with folding it and tearing it into rectangles, on each of which he draws a shape that he then holds up to the light and scrutinizes. Shapes that he likes are put into his pocket, others are scrumpled up and thrown upon the ground.

'He still writes; well, they all do. Keeping up a correspondence, difficult, isn't it?' Dee continues to her friend. 'After a while it all goes phut. Put it this way, darling. I think you reach a point, you know . . . we're women of the world and the world goes round . . . But I'm always pleased to hear from Derek, I will say that. Oh, dreadful nerves, theatrically criss-crossed. I said, "Derek, my love, calm down!" A bundle of nerves. I'd walk into his dressing-room and, well, I'd just know. "Derek," I'd say. "You are not going to do this." Taking the champagne and putting it into my holdall. "Let them come," I'd say. "Let them come by all means. But you, Derek, will be at home with me, eating fish." Oddly, I'd say, with all my lovers, that fish has been the common denominator. Do you know, I'd never thought of that before. Strange, isn't it, when you're talking to someone who really understands.'

The tedium of afternoon has got to Warren, on whose young face there rests an image of despair. Now that the portacabins have been removed there are no classes for the inmates until the original ground-floor rooms that run around the Airing Court are recommissioned. Nothing to do, nowhere to go. Lunch over by one and the long wait till tea and supper and Warren on the eight to eight shift, despairing of his lot. Clouds stack above the court and Warren knows what that means. Little to choose between two evils, standing out here against a wall when he longs to join in with the football or, should it rain, standing in the amplified noise of the vast and galleried expanses of the Wet Weather Room overseeing ping-pong and sponge darts.

"'At the passing of the breeze . . . the holly whistles as it . . .'" Eddie's lips stall on the words and his eye inadvertently falls on Miller. "'At the passing of the holly the breeze trees . . .'" Miller casts a shadow on the wood that Eddie speaks of. "'At the whistle of the fir . . .'"

How he has betrayed them, Miller, that idiot who has let the water in. Miller, the boulder on the path to anywhere; Miller, who stands up above the landscape, the landmark that a messenger hitches his horse to while taking a dekko at the map.

Tall and apparently vacant, unfathomably old, reminiscent in stature and expression – the lack of it – of pictures in old school biology books entitled *Enlarged Pituitary Glands*, Miller strokes the grey striated bark of the walnut tree. Miller, the husk, the disused housing, the bits and pieces taken out of him, the chemicals poured in. Dangerous and cavernous Miller, rusted gear surrounded by blown litter, accompanied by the scraping music of the kicked and battered can. Workings used up, condemned, contaminated; thickets of bramble closing the drawer that was his brain. The props that made the others viable, that held the roof up, are now quite gone. Nicotine-bearded Miller casting a long shadow; wind-tunnel Miller, empty workings, dangerous, barbed-wire Miller, standing head and shoulders high above the others in the Airing Court: insane.

'OK, everyone in. Chop-chop,' shouts Dobie just as Dr Orchid Witty and Miss Gaynor Swift enter the court through the door of Hilversum.

Two women of the same age could scarcely be more different. Orchid is compact, contemporary, dressed in layered lycra, with fine red tights that flash past William Carter, making his weak heart race; Orchid's effective and professional advancing across the court in flat, black patent shoes. Miss Swift teeters in a pair of T-strapped heels, a frilly figure among the hard blocks and corners of the Airing Court, face framed by a floral pie-crust collar reaching to her lower lip.

Miss Swift began the day in pink and at this moment is considerably pinker. Roused to confront Dr Swan on the whereabouts of her soft-toy portacabin, to demand its immediate return, to insist if all else failed that she could not contemplate holding her soft-toy class in any other venue, particularly in one of the old rooms that were held up by pillars and smelt of old brick dust and mice . . . three seconds in the presence of this handsome man and she has given in. Swan has persuaded her that if there is a pillar in the room then she will get around it. 'I know you'll get on top of it,' he said. And she yielded to him, yielded to him, blushed. With Dr Swan at the helm Miss Swift would be reconciled to anything, to teaching in a rat-infested dugout shaken by intermittent shelling. The day looks beautiful to Gaynor Swift as she moons through the Airing Court, almost taking flight on those T-strapped, highheeled shoes.

The patent pumps flash past her, reaching the ragged line of inmates that is Dobie's charge.

'One of these for everyone, Mr Dobie, if you will. One for the Male Attendants' Mess Room. Mr Miller?' Orchid attempts to pass an A4 sheet to Miller but fails to attract his attention. 'Will you take one for Mr Miller, Mr Dobie, please?'

A spatter of rain comes and with it David Davies, the chaplain, rubbing his hands together as if a newsletter from Orchid is exactly what his heart desires.

'It's all about litter,' Orchid says, enunciating loudly as if sheer volume might break the pack-ice that surrounds Miller autumn, winter, summer, spring. 'Our environment,' she says to the chaplain. 'All linked to your proposed mural, vicar. Remember, everybody! The chaplain is looking for recruits!' Spots of rain fall on the papers as Orchid doles them out like boiled sweets.

'The word made flesh,' says William Carter.

'Oh, fuck off!' says Dee.

Eddie marks his page with his sheet. Maisie takes hers and folds it, then leans against the bench and slips it into the toe of one of her wellington boots. Ruck makes his into a paper aeroplane; Dobie takes it from his hands as they go in. At the tail of the line William looks back into the court. Miller is still standing at his post. William looks at him and taps his teeth.

What can it mean, this teeth tapping? Look, I've still got them? Or, If we lose our teeth we're done for? Or, I am William. When I see you I always tap my teeth? Miller doesn't know. He shakes his head and sets the tassel on the fez shivering with frustration. It is these small things that interfere with the large things he must do; small bits and pieces that clog his consciousness. Whatever the answer it rolls away from him, a loose ball-bearing in the stuffed-up, gimballed drawer that is his brain.

A crack of distant thunder comes from the west but Miller doesn't hear it. Alone in the Airing Court he rubs his head against the walnut tree.

Perry & Co.'s Glideaway Nibs: Miller can see the little

box in his imagination. Glideaway. He rubs his head against the tree. A bridge pencil, hard to hold, slim in his fingers, a stub of sealing wax, a bottle of camphorated oil. Luggage labels . . . The thunder retreats still further but the wind gets up before the rain comes. Blue-black ink: how many lobsters will escape the pot? A knife to sharpen a pencil to a point. Miller looks up into the leaves of the Juglans Nigra and feels the first fat raindrops fall upon his throat. As the downpour comes, the smell of wet wood assails him. Glide away . . .

Shifting junk from the Mat and Basket Makers' Room into and on top of other junk in the Uncooked Meat Store, Frank Prennely, senior male attendant and uncle to young Warren, is having a surprisingly fulfilling day. Getting his teeth into a real mess, 'dunging out' as he calls it, is satisfying in itself, but in the course of it he has come across all sorts of things – significantly the twenty four glass cases of the parrot collection – that he hasn't seen for many years. He has got plans for the parrots, but he is keeping them to himself for the moment. For now it is down to work in the Mess Room, where he sits, back to the CCTV monitor, spiking dockets with officious zeal.

Fire slacked down, shirt-sleeves rolled, table cleared. He has got into a rhythm now, pleasantly and usefully absorbed. Somewhere at the back of his head he registers distant thunder, rain on the barred window pane, the misty glow of orange lights. Another noise: a roar, this one, not a rumble. Swinging round in his chair he checks the CCTV monitor.

'Warren!'

That boy is nowhere to be seen.

He goes out into the corridor. No Warren. Dobie is in

the Wet Weather Room, he can see that from the screen but Warren, little blighter . . . Prennely puts his head around the Gents and bangs upon the single door.

'Warren?'

'In here.'

'Get out so as I can see you. For God's sake. Miller's at it. I can't rely on you at all.' He rattles the lock. 'Get out of it this instant, Warren. Out in that court this instant or I'll —'

'I can't, Uncle.'

'What's the matter with you?'

'I feel sick.'

Alone in the court Miller bellows like a cow lowing persistently for a missing calf. Prennely grabs his coat, throwing it anyhow over his shoulders, and shoves out into the downpour. Beyond the water-tower a sheet of lightning whitens the dark sky.

'Right, come on,' he says to Miller, keeping the tone businesslike, keeping the rage over Warren out of his voice. 'Over here. Come on. Let's have you in.' That this situation could so easily have been avoided makes Prennely livid, but the tone he uses remains calm, matter of fact. Like being with a horse, being with Miller, best to keep expression out of your voice. Miller is usually docile; still, Prennely walks and talks in such a way that should there be anyone in the Mess Room – and there should be – they will know he has got the measure of his man.

'OK, Miller, now come on.' The pitch of a familiar voice is often enough to calm him. Though Miller is taller and stronger than Prennely, this afternoon in the downpour he goes where he is bidden, like a little girl. Both are drenched. The bellow has become a low moan that echoes down the hall and far along the corridor. Fat chance that no one else has heard.

Prennely sits the old man down on a grey plastic-moulded chair adjacent to the Mess Room, where he can keep an eye on him, in the downstairs passage that runs from Hilversum to the abandoned Finisterre. He puts a hand firmly on Miller's shoulder to settle him, talking calmly like someone moving the ubiquitous grand piano: 'Left a little. Down. Up a bit. That's got it nicely, steady as we go.' Now he lights one of his own cigarettes for Miller and places it between the man's lips. That should shut him up. The little grey chair is far too small for Miller and as the cigarette comes towards him, his sense of smell, awakened by the wet wood, is confused by other smells: nicotine, Mrs Prennely's washing powder, Mr Prennely's aftershave. The tree wet with rain is what he longs to smell; the tassel shivers on his fez. He bellows, the cigarette dropping from his lips into his lap. Prennely plucks it up smartly and sets it in his mouth. No sign of bloody Warren! You'd think he'd come out if only to see what's going on.

The grey chair faces the wall upon which hangs a large print of *The Sacrifice of Isaac*. Prennely has walked this corridor so many times that he does not see the print at all. Though dockets beckon he stays with Miller until he is satisfied that he has calmed him. Returning to the Mess Room he glowers at Warren and checks the clock.

'You've got a radio, you're a strong lad. What's the matter with you?'

'I feel sick,' says Warren.

'I'll give you sick!'

'I just don't like it.'

'Don't let Mr Dobie hear you saying that. Do you hear me, Warren?' Prennely is too short to shake the boy, but he gives him a push on the shoulder to make his point.

'It's not my fault. I just don't like it,' Warren says.

A big man on a small grey chair, nothing to amuse him but *The Sacrifice of Isaac*.

'Look, there he goes.' Prennely points Miller out to Warren on the monitor. Miller is standing up, nose to the glass-covered print.

'What's he doing?'

'He always does it.'

'Yes but why, Uncle?'

'Well, I don't know.' Prennely lights himself a cigarette. There is wood behind the glass. Miller sniffs the sacrificial pile of faggots, but it is not the smell he is looking for. Sitting down again, Prennely shakes his head. There is no way Prennely can go back to the dockets now, the rhythm has all gone out of it. Nothing but trouble since he was persuaded by his wife's sister to take on young Warren. He fumes in his chair. He would like to stick the spike through Warren and he can't place where he got to in the ledger.

'Watch that screen! Do you hear me, Warren? Watch that fucking screen.'

Fuck indeed; Warren wonders how the fuck he is going to get out of this job.

'Bring him in out of the rain, that's all I asked.' His uncle is not prepared to let this drop. 'Stuff I've dealt with would make your hair stand on end and all I ask . . .'

Warren wonders how he can get his mum to let him work in a factory or something, telephone sales, anything so that he can earn good money, travel, get away. Miller sits immobile on the chair. Watching him, Warren cannot know that he too dreams of travelling, cannot see any change except that the cigarette is finished, that the head has stopped its shaking and the tassel on the fez is still.

With a massive effort of concentration that isn't visible to Warren, gripping the sharp edges of the moulding

43

underneath the plastic chair Miller stares hard and deep at the print upon the wall. He has done it before and he can do it again; with an effort of will he can change *The Sacrifice of Isaac* into the interior of a blue Volkswagen car. Mustering all his energy he can see the discoloured, curved, cream plastic handle set above the glove compartment on the passenger side of the dashboard. The interior of the car is lined in white plastic with minuscule black dots and small, brown, sticky specks of nicotine. He lowers his eyes from the roof of the car and now he sees it, the glove compartment with its chrome push-button. He presses the button and the compartment falls open; inside there is a map.

The car he remembers. Hubert Bottril had something to do with it, but Hubert isn't in the picture because Miller was out on his own. That car . . . Miller remembers how low he had to bend to get himself into it, how he had to stoop. The duck-egg blue of the little car that stopped when he flagged it down. The blue of the car and the purple of the mountain that filled the windscreen.

She was driving in bare feet and the gear-stick between them came out of a black leather glove puppet. It was a gauntlet of a gear-stick. And they were driving towards the mountain in the evening and he knew it was unlikely that they would meet another car . . .

International author, conference star turn, Milan, Cairo and lately Budapest, Dr Swan ensconced, shut away, safe in his sea-green office, thinking.

'No calls, Paula. No interruptions.'

A cordon of peace broken only by thirty seconds of Miss Swift. A shop carnation on a tall straight stem is how Swan sees her. Already his, he knows the signs as clearly as if he had selected her himself from a bucket outside a florists, taken her into his sanctum, crushed her stalk on the edge of a filing cabinet, arranged her on the windowsill to suit himself.

'Well, cheery-bye,' she says pinkly, leaving a smell of lavender behind her.

Renowned authority on mental health care, conference twinkler, lunch was a long look in the mirror and a short drive in the car. After lunch Paula popped her head around the door to say that his father had phoned him.

'Not now, Paula.'

'The Death of the Soul', 'The Birth of the Brain Image', 'Psychic Numbing': one is only as good as one's previous publication. Ideas for future papers stack like planes above an airport, yet at twenty to two and again at fourteen minutes past three – the times are noted in his journal – Dr Swan experiences a slight, but nevertheless perceptible, palpitation from his healthy heart. His current area of research is a backwards look at water treatments, copies of the *Hydropathic Record* and the *Aberdeen Water Cure Journal* are stacked up neatly on his desk. When he straightens the pile his hand is steady and yet – again, when the great bear that is his colleague Dr Beaker lumbers into his office uninvited – his heart flutters beneath his crisply laundered sky-blue shirt.

Beaker is late this morning and late again this afternoon and no doubt when the clock had turned to four he would be slouching out again. A man Swan has tutored by osmosis: never apologize, never explain.

'Dekko at your DP,' mumbles Beaker, referring to Swan's paper on 'Disintegrating Personhood'.

Swan lies and says it is at the binders, thinking only,

delete this hairy man. Beaker leaves the door ajar and Swan gets up to shut it just in time to see the hairiness on the hands of Beaker, hairy hands trundling the trolley of fish. A note in the diary now, Beaker/Fish.

To hood to hide. Swan hasn't written 'Disintegrating Personhood' and it isn't, as they say of failures, that he hasn't tried. His pen had stalled on the little word hood with its images of the Ku Klux Klan and a bag over the head; hood – he couldn't even tease the word out in shorthand. Water cures by contrast hold no horrors, and so he turns his mind to ducking and douching and to Preissnitz, whose heart never palpitated, Preissnitz the head of the first Water Cure University, after whom his native town had named a ship.

Dr Beaker, Beaker/Fish, part of the blip, and Michael Swan could do without him. Beaker lounging in his office, flecks of something or other caught in the hairs of his red beard. Would Beaker get his post today if he were to reapply for it? Beaker shambling in and knocking off; Beaker slopping in his unlaced shoes; Beaker with his flies open; Beaker eating chocolate in his room; Beaker too lazy to talk in anything but shorthand. His sentences are incomplete, flaring briefly then going out like the roll-ups in his ashtray. Beaker who has five children and lives in a stupid house with a Victorian turret; Beaker tearing over the pot-holes in his dreadful camper van. Beaker involved in a tragic accident; Beaker drinking like a buffalo, stomach sagging over the wrinkled waistband of those corduroy trousers. Stressed out, washed up or something more sinister, Beaker the pupil-turned-master overtaking on the inside lane?

Water cures will bring relief. Walking around his room, Swan makes notes into a hand-held tape recorder. 'In Glen Bolcain in Ireland lunatics stood around a lake and smote one another with sprigs of watercress . . .' Drawn to the door he sees slithers of Beaker through the linen blinds. Beaker and Paula, are they talking about him?

'Hole in the sump.'

'What was it last month?'

'Wheel bearings.'

'And pre-ignition. You can say what you like about women and cars but coming all the way out here . . .'

The light burns late in Swan's green glade, while across the Airing Court in the Male Attendants' Mess Room Prennely too works on. Normally at this time of day he would have time to have a read of the paper, but tonight is different. This evening Prennely takes a couple of hundred-watt light bulbs from the store and slips them into his pocket. Singing 'For Those in Peril on the Sea' he grabs a bunch of keys.

Prennely takes the back way in order to avoid CCTV. Through the Upholsterers' Shop walks Prennely, unlocking as he goes. Through the Shoemakers' Shop, the Kitchen Servants' Room and what used be the Cooks' Store, 'O Holy Spirit who didst brood upon the waters dark and rude', back to where he had been working earlier in the day. There were things in here that Prennely hasn't seen for years and years; the stuffed birds – he could have sworn that they had been chucked away.

Prennely fits the new lights and peers at the collection, stacked up any old how, sideways and upside down. Taking a hanky he rubs at the glass of the old display cases. The little pygmy parrot, the three-foot hyacinth macaw. The sulphur-crested cockatoo that hung next to the rainbow lorikeets. Amazons that hung together, white whatchamacallits, African greys – stone the crows, it gives him quite a turn to see them all again. A quiet moment seems called for and Prennely takes it. Standing among the boxes, thinking about Hubert and the old days, the little pygmies are his favourites, like rediscovering old friends.

Fitting the second bulb in the corridor, he can see by the darker shade of brown paint along the walls where the parrots used to hang. Now if he were to shift the notice-board to the other side tomorrow and find a couple of dozen brackets . . . He studies the notice-board: lists for classes, soft toys, calligraphy, pottery, choir, Miller's name – small writing for such a big brute – first on the list for everything. Miller's name is the only name up for the chaplain's proposed mural. Boldly Prennely takes a pen out of his pocket and adds the word 'Snacks' to the chaplain's notice. That might bring them in. Miller! Christ, he has forgotten all about him. Abandoning the parrots Prennely makes a run for it. 'Oh hear me, Lord, I cry to thee, for those in peril on the sea!' On through the dark corridors until he is back by the main entrance to the Mess Room, *The Sacrifice of Isaac*, Miller clinging to the edges of the chair.

No point going home just yet. It is Tuesday and Swan's wife Julia has piano. The department is quiet; Beaker is long gone, Orchid is still in her room, but of course he can't go to her. Paula pops her head around the door. Both of them have forgotten about the message from his father.

'See you in the morning, then. Don't work too hard.'

Alone in the foyer Swan makes himself a cup of coffee, changes the A3 calendar – a present from a drug company, 'We don't,' as Swan so often says, 'live in a perfect world' – from September to October. Orchid. Again the sheen of her hair beneath the anglepoise. No, he can't go in there.

Already dark. Swan draws the blinds and sits thoughtfully at his desk, listening in the silence to the fridge-like hum of his computer. The department clock, all balls and balances, reads sixteen minutes past seven; a time of day he used to cherish for the opportunity to get down to some real work. He pulls one of the journals towards him, but though he fingers the cover with his perfectly manicured hands he doesn't actually look at it. He is lonely and he should feel better for identifying it. It's nothing. Nothing unusual, nothing untoward, nothing that doesn't happen to everybody now and then. Nothing . . . after all, it's nothing, nothing, he is going through a blip.

'It's probably nothing but then you never know, do you?' Dee writes. 'Just to let you know that Bullit is rather off his food. Probably nothing but . . .' Dee rests her writing pad on her knee, slips both shoes off and waggles her toes. Should she call Bullit an elderly dog? That was hardly fair, but if dog years were multiplied by seven or eight . . . 'it's not a good sign, is it, if a dog doesn't want to go out?' The pen slips off her knees. It is late and, sighing a little, she lets the pad slide too.

The television is turned off in the small sitting-room in the dormitory on Roma. Dee considers the cold set and makes a little moue of frustration. Bending awkwardly in her armchair she fishes out her handbag and gets a cigarette. Lighting it, she smokes it just for company. She puts her tired feet up on the table. That's better. Orchid had given her a clothes catalogue, which lies on the table.

'Why don't we have a look through it together?' Orchid had suggested.

'Because I'm far too busy, that's why.'

Dee had quite forgotten the catalogue and now picks it

up eagerly, pushing her glasses up and flicking through the pages. Swimming costumes. There is a spotted black one with a boned top. Dee's mother had her costumes personally constructed for her; she, too, was big on top. Swimming makes her think of Hubert Bottril.

'Poor Hubert,' she shouts to Maisie, who is in the bathroom.

Poor Hubert indeed. Maisie is immersed in washing, prodding and squeezing at a pair of fisherman's socks floating in the scummy sink. Maisie spends hours on her washing, finding comfort in the pummelling and the wringing out. Dee stands squarely in the bathroom in her Chinese housecoat, the sponge-bag over her arm simply an excuse.

'Hubert. I'd pop in a quarter to twelveish,' she says, 'and we'd have a glass of Madeira together. Believe me, darling, those were the days. Obviously he was hitting the bottle, but I'd be the last to blame anyone for that. I said to him, "Hubert. Take comfort where you can get it, dear." He was trying to get his second wife committed somewhere, everybody knew but no one said anything, and in any case he didn't want to talk about it. I brought it up once, but he said he was primarily interested in us and not in bringing his home life into the office. But I said, "Darling, you're trailing it behind you like a cloak!" To my mind it all goes back long before Miller's little . . . escapade. All those years with the first Mrs Bottril so ill, and of course in those days you had to have it all out! So ghastly for him. They'd done everything together. Taking all those slides in foreign countries. They spent more time looking down a viewfinder than they did in bed. But sex isn't everything, is it? And those who think it is should think again.'

Maisie pushes past her with the dripping socks. Only the two of them in here now, what with the deaths, referrals . . . It is cold in the bathroom. Dee washes perfunctorily, a dull pain in her right elbow. Today in the canteen Mrs Brande had to help her tug the ring-pull off a can of drink and Dee had made a fuss about being helped and got ticked off by Dobie. Said she didn't want the drink in any case, claimed that it was flat.

'It galls me, Maisie,' Dee says, drawing up a chair and feeling that twinge in her arm again, yanking the chair as best she can to the side of Maisie's bed. 'Clothes catalogues, outings in her car and enough banging about from the back of Finisterre to make your head spin, and as for the chaplain's bloody mural . . . Maisie, put your name down on that list and you'll answer to me, you know. You'd do well to remember that we don't believe in God. Not God,' she goes on in a different voice. 'No, we don't believe, do we, Bullit? No, darling. Not in doggie heaven, no.'

Maisie has turned her head away from Dee, but she isn't sleeping. Dee drags her chair over to the other side.

'Credit where credits due, that's all I'm asking. I was the one who initiated the entire re-whatsit of that department. Not that I get any thanks, of course. Orchid. What does she know? I can't see what Swan sees in her, can you? All sex, of course. She stood in my way once; I said, "Stand aside, my dear, or I'll black the other eye!" It's not like it was, is it, Maisie? You appreciate that I know. Out they come from university departments, what can you expect?'

Nine fifteen and Maisie is snuffling into her pillow, eyes closed, her skein of dirty grey hair spread out on the bed.

'Hubert was a sweetie,' Dee continues, perfectly aware that she is talking to herself. 'Not sexually active, unfortunately. A bit of a thingy about that. I approached, he declined, but he was awfully sweet about it and that is really the main thing. The second Mrs Bottril, between you, me and the gatepost, Maisie, I'd say she had a personality defect. Oh, he had absolutely no energy left, poor thing! Not a smithereen! I said to him, "Hubert, you're running on empty, sweetheart, take it from me!" A good man. A wife with a personality disorder, not surprising if his ideas were slightly off beam. He said to me that he came out of hell each morning, isn't that awful? He said that PAIN represented civilization. Don't you think that's sweet?'

Dee considers pulling Maisie's hair, a couple of sharp tugs... Abandoning the chair she wanders back to the television, turns it on then turns the sound down, watching dumbly for a little while. Orchid's newsletter on litter catches her eye. She takes it and rolls it up like a scroll, unrolls it and reads a few words. Then, digging into the armchair, retrieves her pen and scrawls 'New lav seat pronto!' across the page of type.

'I'll be in in just a minute, Bullit.'

Toddling back to the bathroom she removes her make-up, tearing yards and yards of loo paper from the roll. Washes with a flannel and then night cream; every time she lifts her arm it hurts. Dee's routine is learnt from boarding school, she could pack for an army if she were asked to, but packing is a talent she can't use. Shoe trees in her small court shoes, skirt and jacket of Mummy's suit hung up. Corset and slip over the back of her chair, tights rolled into a ball, pants and blouse out for the laundry. She smokes her last cigarette in bed and makes a stab at the crossword. At a quarter to ten she puts her own light out.

'Come on then. Up you come. But only if you settle, Bullit. Come on then, darling, come to Mummy. Up you come then, that's it, sweetie. Yes!'

A stiffly folded invitation card to something Miller can't remember has stuck beneath the casing of the drawer that is his brain. Undeveloped film, pipe-cleaner, finger-stall . . . He sniffs thoughtfully. The smell in the corridor where he waits with William Carter – the first two in the queue for the afternoon's soft-toy class – disinfectant. Finger-stall . . . William taps his teeth at Miller. Miller stares, looks long and searchingly at William as if the answer lay upon his face. He tugs at the card in his head but he can't shift it. He shakes his head and moves his weight from foot to foot. And stares.

William mouths the mantra Orchid taught him: 'Put your pain into a triangle until help comes.' William walks away from Miller. Miller follows.

The walls in the corridor are hung with display cases full of stuffed parrots; William has never seen the like before. Miller tap-taps at each case they pass, knocking more than tapping, rapping with his hard old fingers at the large case of the sphinx macaw. As if by knocking hard the door that is his brain might open; as if by tapping he will be brought back to his memory by a sudden shriek or screech; a bill will open, the rasping sound when two claws close upon a branch, the branch will sway and the leaves will flutter . . .

'Settle down.'

In the precious few seconds of quiet that follow Miss Swift's announcement comes the sound of David Davies, chaplain and choir master, 'We'll do this one the twice,' taking singing in the Female Bathhouse. The acoustics are quite good.

'Settle *down*.'

In dribs and drabs, the takers for Miss Swift's soft-toy class wander in and mill about the room.

'Come on, William, I'm not going to eat you,' Dee says, bagging two desks by the window. 'Over here, sweetheart, next to me.'

'Sit,' Miss Swift commands for Miller's benefit. 'I know it's difficult in a new room, just find anywhere.'

But the inmates all had places in the portacabin and they haven't any places here. They're lost. Stupefied by choice and change they stand and gaze about them as if the floor were heaving, as if the room, as William felt it was, were really turning round and round.

'There. There. There. There,' Miss Swift says (losing her temper before she has even started), a hand on each of their heads, sitting them down.

With a familiarity that always irked Miss Swift and that admirably she always managed to fight back, Dee upstages Miss Swift by starting to hand out the needlework. Miss Swift occupies herself with the big blue register. She cannot stop Dee doing what she has chosen to do, but she will not let her dive into the scrap box. She winds a protective arm about it, looks coldly at Dee, and so the daily frustration that she is paid for starts.

Penguin, pig, duck, snake . . . running through the register Miss Swift sees the inmates in terms of the work in which they are presently – it seems endlessly – engaged. Miller – one marked him present though absent would have been more accurate – still on the four-sectioned ball.

'William? William Carter? You're not here to sleep, William.'

'I haven't slept, miss.'

'Well, I'm not . . . oh, sleep if you want to. Now the rest of you, settle down.'

'Did you bring the beads, miss?' asks Verne of the grubby neck brace.

'In a minute. Settle down.'

A class of twelve. She fusses over the register, knowing only too well how once this was done the river would leap its banks, spread everywhere and she, running from inmate to inmate, would be summoned here and shouted at from over there; Miss Swift, with a cloth the size of a hanky, hopelessly mopping up. She had planned to bring the class together at this stage of the course – instruction on eyes and faces – but this group were completely at odds with one another, Miller still on the ball, others way ahead on tails and beaks. She had promised to sew the under-gusset of Dee's piglet. 'You promised me that I'd be first, Miss Swift. You promised me. Me, me, me, me, me!'

Dee is up at her desk again, scrutinizing the register for herself. Miss Swift, aware as she flicked her longish hair over her shoulder of being observed by Warren patrolling the corridor, shoots him a conspiratorial smile through the glass partition: us doing our best to cope with them.

'Settle down.'

Dee, Maisie, Ridout, Fatty Barrett, Verne, Worsem, Applecombe, Miller and William. She has known most of them for years. Knows as much about them as she needs to know to control them, to keep them more or less occupied for three quarters of an hour.

Satisfied with the register Dee pushes her pig at her. Ruck waves his penguin in the air; he had made the wings so small they looked like an afterthought. Attention seekers and sleepers, this is how Miss Swift's class divides. Slumpers who sat each week in silence, who, drugged – she didn't want to know – mooned in and mooned out again each week. Slumpers such as Maisie and William, who never achieved anything, who resisted all attempts to prod them into action, inanimate, 90 per cent elsewhere.

Miss Swift braces herself, draws an upturned and a downturned mouth on the blackboard behind her, reminds the class that the toys they are making might – she doubts it – be bought for children at the Christmas Sale of Work and, if this were indeed the case, why make the little animals look so glum?

'Toys are objects of affection, aren't they? So . . . ,' Miss Swift points to the upturned mouth, 'let's make them happy toys. I'm coming round to see the faces. We must all try and get the faces right.' Was it deliberate intention on the part of some that mades the most genial of creatures look so grim? Only Dee's pig is amiable. Fatty Barrett's mouse, though small, looks more like vermin and Worsem's spotty dog, which she had held such high hopes for, has turned into a nasty cross.

'Better make a muzzle for that one,' Ridout comments.

'Settle down!'

Miller's ball might be attractive if he ever finished it. The colours are good but it has been on the floor and it is dirty. When he passes it to her, meekly, as she stands by his desk she recoils from the feel of it: it is sticky and it smells of Miller, smells of sweat.

'Now eyes really are the key, aren't they?' Miss Swift draws unconsciously the almond eyes of Dr Michael Swan. Quick and beautiful, clear and light. The eyes of the class are Monday at the fishmongers, glazed and dull. Ruck is up again, waving his penguin. 'Remember as you work that someone is going to love this little plaything, want to cuddle it. Very nice, Ruck, now make a start on the wiring of the feet. Eyes are the key to the . . .' Every single time she turns towards the board there seems to be some sort of scuffle going on behind her. 'Settle down! . . . to the personality of the animal and the placing of the eye . . . draw it in . . . lightly with a pencil . . . is vital.'

'Got any black beads, miss?' Verne asks her.

'You don't need black beads.'

'For the eyes, miss.'

'Wait! Now, make sure your animal gets the eyes it deserves.' From the corner of her eye she sees William sleeping. 'Size . . . sit down, Verne. Really, for someone with a neck brace, you're remarkably active. Size . . .' Miss Swift draws a cow on the board and puts a tiny eye on it as an example. 'You see. Give the bead box to Verne. Ridout? Now, do be careful with this,' she says, handing him a drumstick to help with the stuffing of his snake. Dee comes up to her desk again and compliments her on her blouse, trying to stroke it.

'Thank you, Dee. Now. Shall we have a go at your little pig?'

Bright red tights and breasts like little pillows. William isn't sleeping, just thinking about things. About Orchid and Josephine Foxley, about picnicking on the moor-like bosom. A bottle of beer chills in the river that runs along the well field, the well you couldn't see from William Carter's house. William, lying like a rabbit full out in the sun in the valley of her bosoms.

'A friendly object that can be taken to bed.' Miss Swift's comment is greeted by loud laughter. 'A cuddly toy . . . Is there something hard inside this animal, Ridout?'

'He's hardened his heart, miss.'

The laughter irritated.

'Take it out, whatever it is. This minute. I'll take it out!' She ran her seam ripper – 'Oh, miss!' – crossly down the breast seam of the vicious-looking yellow duck. More laughter. 'Now don't let's spoil things by being silly. Settle down.'

Dee presses forward with her piglet. Her teeth are stained with nicotine and Miss Swift would like to knock them down her throat. Dee wants attention and she wants it now. She wants to touch Miss Swift's blouse and to know exactly where she bought it, she wants to talk blouses, jackets, skirts and shoes. She wants to know what is fashionable and how much it costs, right now. She wants to tell

Miss Swift about the boned bathing suit she has ringed in the catalogue. She wants Miss Swift to do her piglet. Now!

'Wait!'

Miss Swift has recently moved house. Rufus Drive, a modern development of starter homes for young families. Miss Swift lives alone.

'How's your kitchen coming on, Miss Swift?' Dee asks her.

'On is not the word.' Gaynor Swift's mind flicks back to an argument with the decorators.' I don't think they listen,' she informs her class.

'You need a husband, miss,' says Fatty Barrett.

'Like a hole in the head,' Miss Swift replies, colouring – pink – as she realizes what she has said.

'Like Miller, miss?'

Miller looked up as his name is spoken.

'Please, everyone. I don't know what's got into you this afternoon. Settle down.'

'Has it got a yard?' asks William.

'No. It's got a patio and raised flower-beds —'

'And a common little washing-line,' says Dee.

When William was young, when he was two and three and four, he stood in the yard with a yellow woollen scarf crossed over his chest under his jacket and he wasn't scared of anything at all. And when he was older he stood on the back of a tractor and braced himself when the tractor pulled up the hill. After breakfast, before school, every morning, he and his brothers foddered the suckling herd that wintered on the downland. Cows pushing up to the tractor, surrounding William with their warm wet noses, long tongues slavering the salt-lick . . .

Fatty Barrett bores easily. The mouse has been discarded. Instead he has taken a feather from Miss Swift's scrap box and cut it up both sides. What a waste of a feather!

'If you don't want to do anything constructive this morning, Barrett, then just sit and be sensible. Ridout, give the wire to Ruck, please. Dee, sit down. Ridout, give the wire to Ruck. He wants to do his penguin's feet.'

'I don't, miss.'

'He must be able to stand up, Ruck.'

'He's for going to bed, miss.'

'Yes, well . . .' Miss Swift thinks of Dr Swan . . .

'He won't be in bed all the time, now, will he?' Miller looms over her. He has taken the stuffing out of his ball for some reason and now he dumps the stuffing on her desk.

'Shall we start again, Miller? Get it right?' Should she take Miller off the ball? Only she could decide. The notion – she'd call it a concept – that one graduated from one thing to another, simply doesn't hold in here. 'Would you like to try something else, Miller?' Miss Swift finds Miller frightening. She stands behind her desk. There is, some-where, a lovely bit of cream bouclé in the scrap box. 'Would you like to go straight on to a sheep?'

'Baa, baa,' someone pipes up. 'Moo, moo.'

Listening to these noises William thinks longingly of death.

Animal noises everywhere, a quack, a squeak, a hiss. Miss Swift ignores it all and puts the scrap box in front of Miller. His hand goes for some organdie.

'A bird or a butterfly? Something with wings?'

Miller drops the organdie on the floor and grabs the spool of wire from the box.

'Can I have the wire, miss?' Verne asks.

'I'm occupied at this moment, Verne.'

'You said I could have the wire, miss!'

'Remember the wire is for feet only.' Miss Swift is watching Miller.

'Or antlers, miss,' suggests Worsem.

'No reindeer in this group if I remember rightly.'

Dee is sulking, her chair turned away from William. She is poking her piglet with a needle, pricking it all over.

'Miller's got the wire, miss,' Verne says.

Miller has the wire, has uncoiled the whole lot of it from the spool and now recoiled it around his wrist.

'Unwind the wire, Miller. Unwind the wire and we'll sort out something for you. Miller!' When Miss Swift snaps he doesn't flinch. 'Unwind the wire and go back to your seat and I'll be with you in just a moment. That's getting on my nerves, Miller, if you don't mind. Unwind the wire!'

'The wire will cut into your flesh, Miller,' Verne says, gloatingly. He likes the sight of blood. 'Miller's hand will come off at the wrist, miss.'

Who cares if Miller's hand came off at the wrist? What difference would it make? Miss Swift fights hard to keep her temper. Any more of this and she will ring the bell.

Fatty Barrett is up now, unwinding the wire.

'Thank you, Barrett. You are sensible.'

'Off his trolley if you ask me, miss.'

'I didn't ask you, Barrett. I've said thank you, now go back to your seat.' Miller makes a bee line for the classroom door and wanders into the corridor to take another gander at the sphinx macaw.

'Miller's gone, miss.' He is brought back in by Warren. 'Miller's back, miss.'

'Yes, thank you, Ridout.'

Back but not back in any sense that Miss Swift understands. He might have been anywhere, though she never wonders where: some netherland beyond the tarmacadamed road?

'You've all played with toys so you know that the sewing must be absolutely secure. Loose stitching is bound to come undone.' Miss Swift holds the snake aloft as an example. 'This sewing is fine,' she says, feeling along it. Her fingers touch a bump. She raises her eyebrows at Ruck.

'He's swallowed something, miss.'

'One way to do it,' Ridout says.

Miss Swift clenches her fists. 'Right, let's have a go at making him a bit flatter, shall we?'

'Tell us about your love life, miss,' Verne says.

'I certainly shall not,' she counters, looking at the clock. 'Now, I want everyone to work together to sort this mess out. Time to start tidying away.'

Miss Swift turns to wipe the board, her tall back to the class, her collared blouse with those little flecks of dandruff, off guard for just a moment, thinking about love.

William snatches the wire and shoves it hard enough into his forearm to produce a stream of blood. Maisie's eyes widen in wonder, Fatty Barrett sticks the feather in his hair, Ridout dabs at William's blood with the cream bouclé, 'Men of Harlech' booms from the bathhouse.

'Everything back in the scrap box, please,' says Miss Swift.

'Cover yourself up, for fuck's sake,' Ridout says to William, pulling the boy's shirt down his arm.

As Senior Male Attendant Frank Prennely took it upon himself to explain things to lesser beings, particularly women, who would not otherwise understand.

'Put it like this, Doreen,' he said patiently to the doyenne of PAIN's canteen. 'They're taking the inside out by propping up the back, right?'

'Doesn't make sense to me, Frank.'

Of course not. Frank lent across the canteen counter and touched her nose with his forefinger. 'Ours not to reason why, Doreen.'

'And Beaker the Squeaker was round there when you went round there?'

'Alfresco as I stand here, Doreen.' Two thirty in the afternoon and Prennely had stuck his nose in at the back of the abandoned Finisterre only to find Dr Beaker poking in a skip. 'Never know what you might turn up,' he had said, yanking at a length of turquoise tubing. Two thirty in the afternoon and Dr Beaker had been drunk.

'You didn't say anything, did you, Frank?'

'I'm not stupid.'

'I didn't mean that, Frank.' Nervously Doreen fished a biro out of her beehive and wrote the first thing that came to mind on the pad that lay upon the counter.

'I'll have that cup of tea when you're ready, please, Doreen.'

The canteen was empty at this time of day. She took Frank's tea down to the table.

'I wouldn't want to upset you, Frank.'

'You haven't done that, Doreen.'

'You're not looking yourself at the moment and I don't mean the jacket.' Doreen hovered.

Sternly Frank sipped at his tea.

'I'll say one thing to you, Doreen, but I don't want it spread.'

'You know I wouldn't breathe —'

'This,' Frank said, making a sweeping gesture with a ginger-nut. 'This,' he said, referring to work in progress on Finisterre, the removal of the portacabins, the erection of the tall sodium lights, the installation of CCTV, the green refurbishment of the psychiatry suite, 'is an insult to our intelligence.'

'Nothing we're not used to, then,' said Doreen boldly, then scampered back to tidy her hair in the little mirror she kept beneath the counter.

Frank lit himself a cigarette and farted. Five minutes passed and then, without even asking, Doreen brought a second cup of tea.

'Carry on any road,' he said, tapping her bottom.

'That's the spirit, Frank.'

Prennely sat back in his chair, savouring the silence. An idea, floating up from nowhere so it seemed, occurred to him.

'I thought I might run a couple of slide shows,' he called across to her.

'That'd be nice.'

'In memory of Hubert.'

Doreen left her tea-cloth on the counter and came out to collect his cup.

'That'd be nice, Frank. Yes.'

It is William's job to clean and tidy the psychiatry suite. His work is meticulous but slow. Each morning before the staff arrives he empties the bins, sprays polish on Paula's L-shaped desk, vacuums beneath it for fluff and fallen paper clips and dusts her photo cube. Discarded paper cups in Beaker's room, full ashtrays; William wipes a cloth across the pictures that show sections of the brain, then sprinkles food on the surface of the fish tank. The fish come bobbing up to get it; sometimes William sits for a while in Paula's chair to watch. With his feather duster he cleans the edges of the vertical linen blinds in each office. In Orchid's room he mists her potted plants. Then he dusts each handle of Swan's filing cabinet and perhaps sits in Swan's revolving chair and spins around. At eight forty-five or thereabouts he leaves the bin bags in the corridor and takes his cleaning trolley up two floors in the lift to the walk-in cleaning cupboard. Here he rinses out his cloths and lingers for a while among the treasures he has stashed away up here, where no one but he can see them, touch them . . . When the gable clock has struck the quarter he stands on a plastic bucket and peers out of the skylight until he sees it, over the wall, beyond the forest, on the horizon, as quick as a fish and as soundless, the glint that he can see on a clear day, of an express train.

'I meant to tell you,' Paula says, grabbing her shorthand pad and cornering Dr Swan before he has a chance to take off his coat. 'I was half-way home and I said to myself, there's something niggling, and I just couldn't put my mind to what it was.'

'I really must get on,' says Dr Swan.

'Your father. Ever such a long message. I had the whole thing down on my pad to give it to you, I don't know how it slipped my mind. He says . . .' – Paula reads from her shorthand, 'that there is no Mr Haircombs in the frame and that Mrs Haircombs is only available for twelve minutes a day (he's timed it, so he says); that he can't eat in the dining-room for fear of falling over' – Paula sneezes, 'Pardon me – and that her car out in front all day is a decoy, for she goes underground to another car and spends all her time in the city, shopping. Which he can prove as there is a picture of her during a bomb scare in yesterday's paper – he doesn't say which paper . . .'

'Go on.'

'His window is the smallest window in the building and from it all he can see is the mound before the motorway and some dismal planting on the bund – If my memory serves me rightly he's mentioned that before? – The only deer that he's seen are in the brochure; moreover,' she draws breath to continue, 'there is only one oak tree and they are not allowed over to it as it has been promised to some Basque separatists who are due over from . . . Guernica? . . . to collect it.'

'His leg's better, then?' says Swan.

In the laundry Eddie walks between the drying racks and one of the windowsills where he has propped his book. 'The lonely lane he was following connected one of the hamlets . . .' To the windowsill and back to the drying rack, rolling a walnut in his hand. 'The lonely lane . . .'

'Are you making me a coffee, darling?' asks Dee.

'The lonely lane . . .'

'Puss, puss, puss.'

Puss, a bastard of a cat from the monstrous marmalade cat family, low slung and heavy, saunters through the open door. This is a cat that objects to being spoken to, let alone picked up, yet Dee makes a grab at him. He struggles as she tries to hold him.

'You're such a wicked man,' Dee says to Eddie. 'What a wicked man,' she says to Puss. Leaving a cigarette burning on the edge of the sink she pours milk into a tin lid for the cat, pouring it deliberately from a height so that it spills over the lip of the lid out on to the floor.

Eddie makes an effort not to notice, not to follow the milk's course as it runs downhill, finding its own level to collects in a dip and form a still white pool. Released, the cat ignores the milk and stalks out of the door. Eddie has forgotten the line, lane, path, whatever; he rolls and rolls the walnut in his palm. Dee stands by him at the window. One hand on the edge of the sill to steady herself, she swings a leg back and forth, back and forth, pointing the toe. Just as Eddie is about to crack she alters her position, standing to attention, smoothing down her stockings, inspecting her shoes, pulling down the hem of her straight skirt.

'Have you got anything for a headache, Eddie?'

'Of course I haven't.'

'But you used to have.'

He ignores her.

'One for you and one for me, don't you remember? I expect you've got something in here somewhere. Is Eddie going to tell Dee where?' She opens and closes the various cupboards that hang above the shallow Belfast sinks. Eddie has a plastic globe that Dee likes to twiddle with, but he has placed it too high for her at the back of the shelf that runs above the washing-machine. She tries to reach it but she can't quite do it, so she reads instead the titles of the library collection he has placed there. She reads in a patronizing way as if it were touchingly pathetic the way that over the years Eddie has attempted to educate himself.

'*Readers Digest Reverse Dictionary, Times Atlas of World History,* A for Apple, B for Bugger, C for Coffee, D for Dog . . . I'll make the coffee if you don't want to. If you're busy . . . You used to let Sheila Henderson make the coffee – why not me?'

Ah, because when Sheila Henderson made coffee for Eddie she was bathing his feet. Every action was an act of love. Female inmates wore blue overalls in those days, not tabards; stiff and shiny nylon overalls. A job lot, the pockets were unevenly placed, making the bodies of their wearers seem lopsided. The first time he had put his arms around Sheila – Eddie remembered how the blue opaque material slipped in his fingers as he searched for her waist – how thin she was, even then. The blue of that material, how it drew him. Her shoulders and her back, he would gaze at her when she wasn't looking, the back of the blue overall that seemed to beg to be touched. Sheila's hand on

66

the drawer knob, tap, kettle, alone together in this elegantly proportioned room; his laundry, how she had hallowed it. Big tins of coffee in those days, grey stuff labelled 'Inter-continental Sweepings'. And she knew how he loved to watch her back and the way the hem of her overall rose when she lifted up her arms. The hand that he loved to watch taking the spoon from the drawer, as he now took the spoon to make coffee for his new companion. How she closed the drawer like a dancer with a nonchalant swivel of her hip and how she closed her eyes when he touched her, when he came up behind her and ran his hands down the back of that static blue nylon. Every bit of chrome reflected Sheila, every bit he polished up. She brought him coffee and she whispered, 'I am bathing your feet.'

Dee has a sewing bobbin in her hand and is attempting to match it perfectly for size with any other small circular point she can discover in the laundry room. 'Too big,' she says. 'Too small. Nearly. Nearly. Small again. Big.' Her glasses swing against her bosom as she joins Eddie once more at the windowsill. Beyond the glass she sees Miller being led across the court by the chaplain. Boldly she places the bobbin between the pages of Eddie's book.

'Verboten,' she states decisively, closing the book on the bobbin, leaning towards Eddie. 'Cuddle me!'

The chapel is chilly and within it the chaplain's voice sounds loud and booming.

'Good of you to spare the time,' he says. 'No point hanging around so let's get started. Now. You do know what you're going to be doing, don't you, Miller? Painting the mural *The Lord Is a Strong Tower*.'

Miller nods his head.

'Now you won't want to get your clothes . . .' The chaplain considers the man before him. And thank you, God, he thinks, for this difficult path, up hill on my hands and knees.

The brick wall has been lime-washed. It is primed, Miller supposes, to begin the proper painting, the painting he is interested in. The chaplain must be unusually preoccupied this afternoon for he makes a sad mistake giving Miller a very large brush and tub of much-diluted emulsion, asking him to go over the wall again. Miller is pretty disappointed with the brush. The chaplain dips it into the paint pot and that loud voice, booming in the empty chapel, talks at Miller about not putting the brush deep into the paint. 'Just the top third of the brush, Miller.' About painting vertically and uniformly and about doing his best, his utmost, not to drip paint on to the chapel floor. The chaplain points to the dust sheet on the floor as he says this, as if Miller were blind, as if he had numbed feet, as if the numbness in his brain extended to his feet, as if he couldn't feel heaven's embroidered cloths beneath him.

Thank you, God, for this difficult path, for the craggy summit hidden in the mist, for the black water boiling in the gully . . . The chaplain hands over the brush and goes up the aisle to the altar steps. He genuflects, then, rubbing warmth into his hands, begins to practise on the organ.

Miller studies the house painter's brush. He doesn't think much of it. With the chaplain's back safely turned he works and works at the base of the bristles, until he has pulled away a hank of hair. This he licks, holds up by the stem, dips it deep into the paint pot and begins to make a mark upon the wall. Without a handle and with such a little, limp hank the work is slow and fiddly. Miller perseveres.

He paints two fine, narrow parallel lines across the wall then stands back to admire them. A path, his path, the wet paint shining out over the dry.

The organ groans and wheezes as the chaplain plays a medley of dirges with remarkable feeling and expression, pumping out the agony with his feet. Miller paints straight on, allowing his path to continue – as it must continue – far beyond the primed white wall. There is no cloth on the floor here and however careful he is, paint drips on to the pews, on to the floor. His path goes through the forest, but this does not hold any fear for Miller, who is exuberant, crashing and braking his way through. Wood pigeons burst into the air at his approach, a bramble flicks back at him, scratching his cheek – only when he stops to dip the hank of hair into the paint pot does he realize that his hands are stiff and cold.

'What in heaven's name! Give me that. What are you doing? I told you –' The chaplain tries to take the hank from Miller; both are splattered with paint as it falls on to the floor. 'I told you. If you want to take part then you do what you're bloody well told!' The chaplain puts his hand over his mouth, stopping any further blasphemy, marking his lips with white. 'I'd rather not lose my temper,' he says. Bending down to pick up the hank, however, he loses it again. 'I went over the wall myself, Miller, with a roller and I asked you to go over it again with the brush. Deferred gratification, Miller, like heaven,' says the chaplain, profoundly doubting if Miller understands. 'Like heaven,' he booms, 'the pay off comes later. Two coats!'

Two coats . . . I went over the wall myself . . . two coats . . . the phrases resonate for Miller so he hangs on to the pew in order to think it through, paint smearing on to the back of the pew. He must sit down and think about two coats. Heavily he sits, holding the big brush. The chaplain closes the organ with a bang. Two coats because it's cold out there and the weather comes at you from the back.

Now the chaplain walks around his church, past the christening font (unused), touching the church furniture as he passes. The lectern, the font, round and round and round. He won't look at Miller in case he loses his temper. Instead he walks to the door and looks out into the shadowed Airing Court. Puddles of rain turned orange by the sodium lights, lights from windows, lights from the psychiatry suite. Orchid and Swan, as rampant as fed horses in the morning . . . Returning at last to his charge he takes the brush and begins repainting, obliterating the painstaking path, a swathe of white over white. Miller sits and watches.

Before the bell can ring the chaplain takes Miller into the chaplaincy and stands with him – Miller smell and Turps smell – as Miller cleans himself up. How thoroughly the old man washes his big hands once he gets started, like a child showing how good he is at doing it himself.

'Take one,' he says, seeing Miller eye a bag of sweets on his mantelpiece. 'Have a couple.'

Now the Airing Court is full of noise, inmates entering from different directions, gathering to be chaperoned to tea, clustering out of the rain, taking shelter in the doorways. Dark already this afternoon and raining hard.

'Why not wait here until the chaperones come?' the chaplain suggests, and so they stand in the narrow hall by the open door. 'Look. I do apologize for losing my temper, Miller. We've broken the back of it now and once that coat is dry . . . come back tomorrow and we'll get on to something more interesting.' On impulse he takes Miller's clean hand in his own hands and holds it for a moment.

'Chop-chop. In a line. In a line,' comes the voice of Mr Dobie. The chaplain would like to say something more to Miller but there is nothing to say.

The soul, if it exists, is lighter than William's hands, hands so cumbersome that he cannot turn in bed. It is friable, though the edges are securely sewn with infinitesimally tiny diagonal stitches; it turns when you turn, it tilts when you tilt, but it keeps the shape of an exquisite oval. An island that William sketches on squares of grease-proof paper, oval souls identical for everyone, measuring precisely two inches from tip to tip and one inch and a half across its widest point. Insubstantial, melting in the hand like snow. Up and up the soul goes, caught in the thermals of the four blocks of the Airing Court, and they're clapping, someone's clapping, Dobie's clapping.

William hasn't slept, but those who have are now waking. William lingers, thinking of the soul that melts like snow but lighter and whiter, as white as a leg beneath blood-red stockings, as white as the pillow of Orchid's breast, as white as the hand that taps into the keyboard, notifying nurses 'Instructions for October', withdrawing medication from William Carter, gram by gram, stage by stage, step by step.

William's hands are so enormous that the weight of them in bed woke him. They look normal but they aren't normal, they are steady but somehow solid hands. Painfully he gathers his clothes into a bundle, drops a shoe and leaves it, dashes towards the lavatory, leans against the wall to wait for a free one, bursts in and leans again against the door. His hands aren't working; he cannot slide the bolt to lock the door.

Shirt, no; socks, no; he cannot even tie his shirt around

71

his waist. Jumper next to his skin, shirt pushed into the waistband of his trousers; trousers round his ankles, shirt now on the floor of the lavatory.

'For fuck's sake!' Fatty Barrett bangs on the cubicle.

'Get me Ridout,' William urges. After a long time Ridout comes in, goes again and then comes back with tracksuit bottoms.

'Can you hold your dick?' asks Ridout, who has seen this sort of thing before.

William tries it.

'Put it back in then. God almighty!'

Hungry but William can't risk eating. He is ashamed of his condition. Nobody must know. Warren is on duty in the canteen and is busy changing the tape in his Walkman.

'Good?' asks William.

'Depends what you like, doesn't it?'

'What do you like?'

'I'm not meant to listen, really,' admits Warren.

'Rough.' William longs, just longs to sink into a chair but knows that he can't risk it. He must stand up. It must appear that he has eaten his breakfast.

'What do you like?' Warren asks.

'I don't know.'

William can't roll a cigarette in this state – O God deliver him. Slipping past Warren he makes it through the canteen door and into another lavatory. Now he clamps his right hand over the cold tap, struggles, wrenches, turns on the tap and puts his hands and then his whole face and head beneath the water. The skin of his scalp feels paper-thin, dots of headache just beneath the surface, tongues of flame.

Beaker is on Sunday shift, sitting in the Wet Weather Room with his bleeper on, reading an instruction leaflet on how to make a one-man canoe. One of the marmalade cats threads through his spread-eagled legs. William, big hands on his lap and simply sitting, watches the cat as it sniffs in the room's four corners. How the cat's tail sways, how it presses itself down on to the bare floorboards. How patient it is, how willing to wait for the right moment.

The Wet Weather Room is cold and noisy. Someone has tried to mend the pool-table pockets with netting from a bag of oranges. The balls fall regularly through the holes, bouncing loudly on the floor. Maisie sits sewing by the window, her slippered feet out in front of her; Eddie reads in front of the television; Ruck has taken his chair right up to the set, where he watches intently, bending forward.

Three thirty and Beaker is free to go, a half-hour drive that takes him through the forest, coming home to chaos and getting straight into it without removing his coat. Throwing bathing suits accurately at a rack above the radiator, frying waffles, talking a child through the intricacies of cinema booking over the phone. Tracing a map of South America for the eldest, bringing the logs in, making two milkshakes, drying some spark plugs with a hairdryer, sliding the waffles on to a plate.

As the inmates are led outside to the Airing Court after tea, Beaker hollers into his wild back garden, calling and calling into the twilight for the straggling band of children out collecting conkers.

In PAIN it is 'Everybody out! Come on. Chop-chop,' with Dobie giving the orders at the double. Out they go, as the rooks fly in to settle on the water-tower. Dee with Maisie; Hobbs, who hasn't been around for sometime and looks peculiar; Ruck, Verne and Barrett; Feltham with his hands clasped high up his back.

Dee looks different this evening. A pink cardigan, far too small for her, is perched over her shoulders, pink clashing against the orange of her tabard, both colours bleached as she passes back and forth beneath the sodium lights.

'I told them till I was blue in the face, but you can't tell them anything. I said, "This poor little woman, one of my dearest friends . . ." Did anyone pay any attention?' Ash from her cigarette grows long and falls into the folds of her Sunday skirt. Moths fly beneath the lights, catching Maisie's attention. '"If you're determined to do it," I said. "Do you need this cardigan? Joke, Sheila! It's not your colour; I like it," I said, "but it's not really your colour, is it?" I said. "You, Sheila, are drained by a yellowy pink. If it's got to be pink then a pink from the blue family." Of course, it was simply ghastly, and my fault entirely. I should have known, but then one is so busy, Maisie, don't you think? Hardly time to turn around.'

The soul turns, but William is hardly going to mention it, not to Eddie, or to Orchid or to Dr Swan. Turning and forever twisting like weed beneath the surface of deep water, presenting one face and then another, indolently moving with the flow.

'"Yes, I'll take over from Sheila in the laundry if that's what you want me to do, but then you can't turn round and make me responsible for Eddie's actions, the actions of a full-blooded, highly sexed man. Wait," I said, "Stop, think," I said, "listen and look." Sheila was flashing like a Belisha. Everyone knew it, Maisie, I said exactly that to Dr Swan. "But you can't see a great deal from up there in your department, can you, doctor?" That got him. He went quite pink. When asked to give evidence I said that everyone on Roma knew, well, they'd seen her do it, heard her, they'd smelt it, and her teeth were terrible. She was sicking everything up! It was only a matter of time, for God's sake,

any fool could have seen it coming. All over the papers, of
course. I don't like journalists any more than you do,
Maisie, look what they did to Tony Hancock. When Sheila
said, "Do you want my cardigan?" I said, "Well, Sheila, it's
hardly Norman Hartnell, but since you're offering." The
body weight of a feather, Maisie, we're talking feather-
weights. I didn't lend her anything, she took that belt. "If
you don't, or won't, come into Roma, then you're not going
to know. And if you won't ask people who do know . . ."
You see, that's just it and none them can face it. They won't
ask us and if they asked us, well . . . I for one would have
been more than happy to point them in the right direction.
Cushions from the TV Room stuffed into every orifice. No,
of course I don't mean that. I'm only saying, Maisie, that
towards the end she was really padded out. For months.
Poor little thing, going off to the WC and fainting. It may
sound hard but I'm telling you, she was like a skittle,
sweetie. I just can't believe that no one knew.'

Dee taps a fresh cigarette, counts through her packet
and then decides against it. 'I was a special friend, but I am
not a lesbian, thank you very much, and if you want that
verified then just phone Derek Jacobi. *"Prenez garde,"* I
told them. "You won't get away with it for very long." And
in any case, what goes on in a woman's ward in one of these
places is nothing to do with the likes of you. If you're so
worried about clittorissimos then go and talk to the
Muslims." That shut them up. "Muslims, pronto. I don't
need to spell it out. You can leave me to my grief," I said,
"and if you want to talk to someone in authority I suggest
you do your own fancy footwork. And if you ask me where
I think you ought to make a start," I told them, "then try
the second floor of Hilversum, up the central stairs."'

A screech owl calls, a walnut drops, at Beaker's house children squabble on the landing as one of them steals a second turn at sliding down the stairs. Time for slaps and threats of a total moratorium on television. Beaker speed-reads a story about an elephant then wallows in the bath with his specs on, gouging small bits of coloured Lego from the soap.

Round and round and round go the inmates in the Airing Court, falling into step and silence, a reverie of walking, so that they barely realize that the hour is late, out in the darkness, under the lights. Silence in a place where there is precious little silence. Patience settles on this evening locomotion. Miller opens the drawer of his head and takes out a bus ticket. With this he walks around, the tassel hanging limply from his fez. Not a sneeze or cough, only the sound of Maisie's tipped stick tapping.

The clock strikes seven but it feels like no time. William, virtually sleep-walking, floats on the water underneath the orange lights. Relaxed and easy, just letting the tide take him, walking arm in arm with Eddie. Here in the company of others the horror of his hands sheers away like ice breaking from a berg and William has the sense that time, so different for each of them and usually so isolating, has now somehow, this mild late-autumn evening, joined them to one another. He is not alone, he is part of the together, linked up with the present and also with the past. Something in this court tonight defies all chronology, walking somehow loosening the bricks between one inmate and the other, the present and the past, the now and the then.

'Like looking at a river in a city,' William says to Eddie. William in the city wearing his pink, buttoned-down collar, fitted shirt, his high-heeled boots. All of it yields to nothing; he won't say this to Eddie. Walking wipes the mind – do hibernating animals feel like this? This must be the time of low body temperatures, a type of walking tortoise/dormouse sleep. A peace that isn't sought or ambushed, that comes up through the asphalt as he walks, hanging on the arm of his big friend. William holds the arm and wants to stay like this for ever; holding the arm and shortening his step to Eddie's will keep him safe.

The buttoned-down collar of the shirt comes from the other life, as do the reflections of street lights in the river. It comes from the years when the gate closed on the farm, when William bought the leather-look jacket with the inside pockets and the high-heeled, zipped-up boots. Years between seventeen and twenty, when the months that passed were not like other people's months. Then the seasons and the months were spaced like stepping stones set too far apart and William tried and failed to get into his stride. Either he fell into the water or his young legs leapt, startling himself, from April into August. Then he was under the mesh in the big city – or that was how it seemed to him. The mesh sagged just above his head and he couldn't see the sky or feel the sunshine. And after this came the cold that the jacket was no match for, a 2 a.m. bone cold that reached to his fingertips and started with a tightening, almost a clenching, of his chest. It fixed upon his senses. He leapt across the true green of spring and missed it, so that cold was followed by six months of August, back under the dirty web of sagging mesh. A mesh that was alive and continually buzzing. August was a furred tongue without any breeze to break it. Now, holding Eddie's arm, he wanted badly to go in at once to the dormitory, to lie down and sleep, but Eddie was against it – or that was how it seemed to him.

Prennely lives in a tied house on the campus. It is a five-minute walk and if he leaves home at twenty to eight he is up at the asylum with time in hand to sort himself out before his shift starts. A walk that gets brighter and brighter as he approaches the buildings, for these days PAIN is lit up like a motorway roundabout, a stage.

Warren has attached counterweights to one of the lockers and is working on his arm muscles. Prennely looks from him to the CCTV monitor and hits the roof.

'I don't believe it! Get them out of that damp air! Put that ... paraphernalia ... you've no right to bring that stuff ...'

'Chill out, Hitler.' The boy moves slowly.

Prennely watches the screen until the court empties. Satisfied, he puts his sandwiches on the side and smoothes out the evening paper. Rolling up his shirt-sleeves, slacking the fire down, he reflects on what a mistake it always is to do someone a favour. For Warren is not and will never be good at his job. The conversation that might run, 'If you want to keep your job you've got to brace up, Warren' or threats of 'last in, first out' are simply pointless as Warren doesn't want to keep his job. At the back of his locker Prennely keeps a half-bottle of brandy. He takes a nip. It is then he sees her on the monitor, just for a moment, there one minute, gone the next, this revenant: a little woman in a long grey apron, orange light playing on a dark face that is framed by the ties of her white cap. A small cretin with a bird-like head, coming through the door from the orchard with apples in her apron, setting out to cross the Airing Court.

If Swan should ever be asked to speak in mitigation he would claim that the coldness of his wife had propelled him towards all those extramarital affairs. A stickler for chronology might argue on the other hand that Julia's coldness was a result of Swan's philandering and not the cause of it . . . whateverwhichway round Swan considered on the train back from his latest conference that he might just be coming through the blip. No ship as yet had been named for Swan but a beguiling red-headed neuroscientist he had met in the hotel lift persuaded him that it was only a matter of time. Swan could pride himself on rekindling an interest in spas: 'Yukons, where the water sparkled with gold. Every dawn the hills were alive with earnest water drinkers, often in curious undress, carrying drinking horns and clumping along with the aid of alpenstocks. By ancient St Anne's well . . .' Twenty-four hours away from home and he felt good. A successful paper, an exuberant night but the journey back was marred by an encounter. A tramp with a torn brown paper bag on his head, who had clutched at Swan's briefcase as Swan stepped from his taxi into the station. Swan slept on the train, the redhead becoming, in that peculiar way of dreams, Mrs Eversley, his father's keeper from Eventide. He awoke with a start then fell back to sleep to dream again. This time he found himself sharing a hotel bedroom with Margaret Thatcher. 'Hop to the bathroom, Michael,' she ordered and he had hopped to please her. Actually it would have been difficult to have done otherwise as his pyjama bottoms had been bound to his ankles, lengths of baling twine wound around his legs.

William is brimming. A geyser of bubbling hot water pulses in his abdomen, great spurts of water up his legs and down his arms. Only where his head meets his neck is there a valve that is working. His head, screwed on to his neck, keeps the water level down. If he curls his toes to stop it coming, in seconds his fingers tingle and fill up. In this state he misses breakfast then whizzes around the psychiatric department in record time, dusting, vacuuming, feeding the fish as if it were all one seamless motion. Closing himself into the lift when the work is done he walks round and round his cleaning trolley. Each time he reaches the ground floor he goes straight up again, everything and anything bent to the effort of working off his energy. On the third descent he thinks he's ready. Pushing the heavy lift door with one hand, then pushing the trolley, again one handed, all the way round the ground floor of Hilversum, through the flap doors where Miller is made to sit and gaze at *The Sacrifice of Isaac*, down to Roma and then all the way back. Miss Swift passes in conversation with the chaplain and William is taking no chances. He stands bent over as if to right one of the castors on the trolley and as he bends his whole body feels simultaneously fluid and wrought. Running up the hill at home, harnessed to the tractor, he wants to run, run but he knows that he dare not do it. Whatever he does someone will be watching, even if he were to rub his hand over his eyes in the frantic way he longs to, someone will see him, touch a buzzer, ring a bell.

It is easy to nod your head when your limbs are shaking. William nods his head at Mrs Brande in the canteen. Nods as she turns the hot plate on and tells him tales of her son Christopher: he might be excluded from school at the moment, but he still needs something warm in his stomach to start the day. 'And will he wear a coat? Of course not, right down the road as far as petrol station in just a T-shirt and a pair of jeans.' The only history in her house is that of Christopher's weak chest, a battlefield strewn with discarded duffle coats, proper woollen sweaters, long-sleeved vests . . .

Fried food to pack on top of the water, to keep the water down. As William eats he feels the water inside him cooling and receding. He can't taste anything but he knows it is working and by the time he has finished he cannot only agree with Mrs Brande that he was just like Christopher – perhaps he is Christopher? – but he can almost see the words she's saying, the length and shape of each word as it comes out of her mouth.

'Hello, sweetie,' Dee calls to William from the laundry.

'Are we baking any bread today?' Mr Dobie asks.

'Just getting a fresh apron,' William says, checking that he is not wearing one already. Dobie heads back towards the Mess Room. Dee is patting a place beside her on the sewing bench.

'Come on, William. Over here. I absolutely insist.'

She pats his thigh, raising her eyebrows to take in Eddie. 'These things are sent to try us.' Removing her hand from his leg she takes her lipstick from her handbag and applies it, looking into the chrome of her sewing machine, pursing her lips and replacing the cap on her lipstick. Everything to William seems this distinct, this slow. She blots her lips with a stray piece of material.

'I haven't had a good day at all,' says Dee.

The apron is forgotten. How warm it is in this laundry, sitting next to Dee.

'Noticed anything different about me this morning, Eddie?' Dee smoothes the faux pearl buttons on Sheila's cardigan and gives herself and the cardigan a reassuring pat. 'Eddie?'

'What?'

'I said, have you noticed anything different?'

Eddie looks at her and shakes his head.

'Sheila's cardigan!'

Eddie recognizes it.

'Happy days,' says Dee.

'Sheila didn't hang around to be gassed,' Dee tells William in a loud voice guaranteed to reach across the room. 'We all thought Eddie was taking care of it. Taking care of her, I mean. Everyone was talking about it but personally I thought it . . . indelicate. Sadly, even as an adult – and you'll learn this, William, it will come – one is so often wrong. Such a selfish thing to do, quite obvious to anyone with the slightest intuition that there just wasn't anything substantial enough – I mean a relationship, William – to tie her to this world. The clang of the death bell, doyng, doyng . . . Funny, I was thinking only the other day how long ago it seems. Not that you forget, of course, isn't that right, Eddie? Someone who has set themselves the task of remembering things isn't likely to forget, William. Eddie wouldn't want to forget Sheila, unless of course he blames himself.'

Eddie gets himself to the laundry door and walks out into the Airing Court. Before the cold air can calm him, Dobie brings him in.

An uphill struggle this earthly pilgrimage; the shaly surface of the mountain is slippery underfoot and the chaplain's god would like him to do it in a pair of Miss Swift's high-heeled shoes. Though David Davies would much prefer to stand by his little buzzing fridge in the chaplaincy and dip his finger into a jar of chocolate spread streaked with peanut butter, he mingles in the canteen.

Ridout has put his name down for the mural. More useful than Miller but Davies is wary.

'I could do hell standing on my head,' says Ridout.

'That won't be necessary.'

'What is it you want, then, vicar?'

'Well, a tower, Ridout, a strong tower. Crenellations, fortifications, buttresses. Something in a good position, on a hill; something symbolically reaching upwards, breaking through the cloud cover . . . angels, possibly a cherub or two, beams of sunlight reflected on golden trumpets, flags, banners –'

'No hell at all, then, vicar?'

'No, Ridout.'

'Not even a little bit of it close to the skirting?'

'Absolutely not.'

Once the chaplain has moved on, Ridout stretches from his table to the one occupied by William and Eddie.

'You should come along,' he says to William. 'Snacks.'

'Budge up,' says Fatty Barrett, trying to join them.

'This table's taken,' Eddie says.

An image of Sheila's soul occurs to William: those little diagonal stitches, the sort of stitches of which Miss Swift would approve, but all coming undone around the edges. If there is a soul, then Sheila's soul, the soul of a suicide, is unravelled, imperfect in the eyes of God and damned.

Dobie walks backwards through the tables. All around them is the din of the canteen at lunch-time, tin plate on tin tray, tin tray on tin trolley. Maisie's stick is propped against her chair. She wolfs her food while Dee, by contrast, picks through hers, examining every morsel.

'Find a seat and sit in it, Barrett,' Dobie says. 'Chop-chop. I won't tell you again.' Dobie backs into the chaplain and the chaplain apologizes. 'Get on with it, Barrett. For God's sake!' continues Dobie.

Miller slurps his soup and William hears the slurping distinctly underneath the general din, sees the stain of spaghetti sauce on Ridout's cuff, spreading, orangey red. Fingers wiped on trouser legs, roll-ups stubbed out in saucers, the skein of Maisie's dirty grey pony-tail. Rank, rank, the colour of a sodden pavement.

William has grabbed Eddie by the wrist.

Eddie puts his fork down. 'Let go,' he says.

William apologizes.

Rank. The half-living and the dead kicked into a hole by Maisie's cut-off wellingtons, scraped into the sluice bucket with a flick from Mrs Brande's spatula . . .

'You're doing it again,' says Eddie.

William takes his hand off Eddie's arm.

Eddie memorizes between mouthfuls, 'All the evidence of his nature were those afforded by the spirit of his footsteps . . . the lonely lane he was following . . .'

Miller listens to Eddie. Listens hard. He pushes his soup to one side and taps his head reflectively with his spoon. Listening.

' . . . the spirit of his footsteps . . .'

Footsteps beyond the crashing and the braking of branches that is the forest? Footsteps that tap along a lonely lane. Tap, tap, tap on his head with the spoon as if to knock the message in securely, to put the nail in true, to hold the sentence so that he may consider it and reject if he needs to, when he wants to, should he choose to, when he bloody well sees fit!

There is so much noise in the canteen. Clash goes the cover of the container of mashed potato. Miller drops his spoon, adding to the noise around him, and holds fast to the seat of his chair.

'Uuuh,' he moans involuntarily. 'Uuuh, uuuh.' Like a woman giving birth, he doesn't think he is going to be able to do it, he can't do it, that last push. He must get out of the noise at once with the sentence intact, he must get outside to hear the sentence again. Miller gets up and strides towards the nearest window and points, moaning, 'Uuuh! Uuuh!' into the Airing Court.

'You can go out in a minute, Miller,' Dobie says, approaching. 'Wait till after lunch.'

'Uuuh! Uuuh!'

'Sit down and have your pudding.'

Miller shakes his head. The bars of the window come up to his shoulders. Like a child standing in a cot he holds on to the horizontal bars in front of him, moaning and trying to pull himself up.

'Give it a rest, Miller,' says somebody.

Ridout pipes up, 'Give it all you've got!'

The chaplain fiddles with his shoelace. There comes a chorus of 'Sit down!', 'Shut up!', 'Wanker!'

Miller is absolutely terrified that he is going to lose the sentence if he doesn't get out immediately. His grunts become more frequent, more urgent, louder.

Dobie comes up behind him, calling for assistance on his radio.

'If you make that sort of noise you won't be going outside, do you hear me? Do you hear me, Miller? Now go over there. Sit down. You don't have to eat your pudding if you don't want to, just sit down until everyone else is ready. Sit down or you won't go outside. Is that clear?' Dobie unclenches Miller's hands from the bars and takes his arm. Miller allows himself to be led back to a table, any table.

Too much noise. Miller sits and trembles. The moment has passed and with it the sentence.

'Sixty chairs, Warren, set out in rows of ten.'

Prennely's nephew chucks the chairs on to the floor. Prennely picks them up, dusts them off, straightens the backs and adjusts the distance between them. The high stool for the slides and the green baize table for the projector.

'Take it back to the far wall, Warren.'

Every third Wednesday, that is how it used to be in the old days. The backcloth when Prennely unfolds it – he had folded it carefully himself, how many years ago? – was hardly creased, hardly faded.

'Do I let them in or what?' asks Warren, lugging the screen and the slide box.

'Leave that lot.'

Every third Wednesday. The very phrase has a magic for Prennely. He simply cannot understand why his nephew doesn't feel the same. There was, is now, a system, a procedure, guidelines to follow, precedent. Inmates are not allowed in until precisely quarter to seven.

'Sixty chairs, not sixteen, Warren, and don't start too close to the screen.'

'Like school,' says Warren bleakly.

'Now this goes up no trouble at all . . . slides here, tape recorder here, stool there . . .'

'X marks the spot,' says Warren under his breath.

Dee is quite dressed up this evening. She is wearing one of Mummy's old Tricosa suits.

'Over here, darling,' she waves to William. Miller lumbers towards her. 'Not you, idiot!'

'I want to show you this,' she says to William, opening her jacket and revealing the pink cardigan. William is breathing heavily as if he had run all the way around the block, 'Symbolic,' Dee says, squeezing his cold hand. *'In memoriam,* you know . . .'

This evening William looks almost as distracted as Miller; clothes flung on, tabard undone and slipping from side to side.

'You shouldn't race about so much, darling,' Dee says. 'You're going the right way to tiring yourself out. You're quite out of puff now, aren't you? Bugger, there's Orchid, on whose permission may I ask? Names, I'd like a list please. Who permitted her to come in here?'

'I'd like a chair if that's possible,' Orchid says to Warren, who ignores her. 'You're looking very smart this evening, Dee.'

'Warren will do anything for me,' Dee says pointedly, turning her back on Orchid, 'Would you like the window open, William? Warren, Warren, over here! What you've got to remember, sweetheart,' she says to William, 'is that at your age you're probably still growing and you don't want to outgrow your strength now, do you?' She puts her hand upon his knee. 'I knew you'd understand about Sheila,' she whispers. 'The cardigan, you know. Though there are more than one or two who'd say, "Why bother?" Mentioning no names, William, mentioning no names . . . It's true she came from a very undistinguished background – her hair was dyed – but you can't judge a book by its cover, William, especially in here. Maisie's rather of the same ilk, I'm afraid, let's put it this way – Eddie!' Dee calls across the room. 'Eddie! Over here.'

Prennely doesn't want Orchid around either, he wants everything to be just as it was. Ridout used to run the slides and it all went like clockwork. 'I'll leave things in your capable hands, then, Ridout,' Prennely says. 'Ready for me to flick the switch?'

Ridout presses 'Play' on the tape recorder and puts the first slide in, signalling for Prennely to extinguish the lights. Even Dee stops talking.

By those in authority Hubert Bottril is remembered with horror. His file is edged in black, marked by charges of negligence, inconsistency, forwardness, backwardness, unfitting behaviour – drunkeness – while being in charge of an asylum. The last page of the file, red, as if a large and squelchy jam sandwich had been pressed against the paper, records Bottril's last and most inappropriate project. The – unsupervised – digging of the swimming pool Dr Swan can see from his office and Miller's escape into the surrounding forest armed with a sturdy garden spade.

Inmates tell a different story. Ridout remembers him fondly for turning a blind eye to a set of funerary urns made in the pottery class. Maisie remembers his watercress treatments for her legs. Fatty Barrett appreciated his extensive knowledge of sport, particularly cricket. Like Jesus he left them rather suddenly, but like Jesus he left them a ritual to remember him by. The slide collection and Hubert's accompanying taped lectures: 'Beachcombing', 'The Great Fossil Hunters', 'Connemara by Pony and Trap' (his first honeymoon), 'Treasures of the Great Barrier Reef' (his second honeymoon) and 'A Visit to the North-West Territories'. The last two sets of slides became muddled when Verne stood in for Ridout. If anybody noticed, they haven't made a fuss about it yet, for on those autumn Wednesdays what the inmates turn up to the Wet Weather Room for is Hubert Bottril's voice.

Slightly hesitant, hopelessly aristocratic, his voice is redolent of the idiosyncratic behaviour that got him into so much trouble.

'A bit of a pickle,' as Dee fondly says. On those evenings it is not what Hubert says but the way he says it. If he had made a tape that began, 'Here is one of my three grey suits. This is the pocket, this is the button hole,' all would have been equally enamoured. If he had taped, 'Once in 1963 I lost my bus ticket,' they would have gone along with it, all the way. Unique among chief medical officers of PAIN, here is a man as interesting as the inmates in his care.

No call for silence is needed in the room tonight. The sound of Hubert's recorded voice zips William straight into a duck-down sleeping bag complete with sheep hot-water bottle with four soft black satin legs. Miller, who regularly confused Hubert with the Saviour, leans forward in his chair attentively, hearing 'Leave your nets and follow me.' As Dee listens the irritation of Orchid's presence is forgotten. Dee's body is transformed and her face made radiant. Hubert is the mirror that reflects her as beautiful.

'In 1976 I and the first Mrs Bottril travelled on the HMS *Devonia* to spend six weeks in the North West Territories of Canada . . .'

William's breathing becomes slow and rhythmic, the loved child with the stamp collection and plenty of pocket-money, swinging between the arms of Hubert and his wife. Dee basks, Miller's forehead is anointed.

'The migration of the caribou herds . . .'

The last time Eddie heard this he was here with Sheila Henderson. They sat together at the back. She had taken off one of her shoes and socks and he had lifted her foot into his lap and he was so grateful for it in the darkness. It was like a dream to hold that foot and he thought that he would never, ever, be able to face the intimacy of the rest of her body. One foot was enough, though enough is never enough. This little foot that felt white in the darkness, that had hammer toes and was warm and he could stroke it and put his fingers between the toes and he could cradle it and rock it. The Airing Court was dark at night in those days and Eddie could look out at the stars . . .

'Churchill or Kennedy,' Dee says dismissively to William in the break. 'May I ask why this sudden interest in funerals?'

'Did the horses have black ostrich feathers?'

'You remember, don't you, Miller?' taunts Dee.

And Miller does remember something.

'Cigars.'

Eddie holds his hands in his lap. Thwarted hands that are terrible, big and strong; a big hand to put over Dee's mouth and shut her up for ever.

Hubert worshipped the first Mrs Bottril; he made sure that at least her arm was in shot for every picture. Hubert's commentary speaks of the waste of lives in the Goldrush. Mrs B. is there with him in Dawson City, her arm indicating the restored Klondike Hotel. The next slide is of the Hudson Bay Store at McKenzie with Mrs Bottril's arm in the foreground, dangling a mink trap. Though this slide is followed by a shoal of clown fish, Eddie gets left behind in Canada, in the North-West Territories of his affair with Sheila Henderson. He chips the ice off their little cabin window and looks out on to Great Slave Lake. They have eaten the last of the dog team and all they can hope for now is a passing Jesuit . . . if they are going to make love it is now or never . . .

Dee snorkels gaily in the blue sea off the Great Barrier Reef. Given the lack of evidence to the contrary William decides there is a soul, decides that the metal workers' mask he has in his pocket is as close as he can get to its gauzy substance. He turns the mask over in his fingers. The gauze is treated so it will not fray.

'No need to hand sew anything for souls,' he says, passing the mask across Dee to Eddie. 'Just cut this stuff into an oval. They come in packs of twelve, so twelve by twenty-five . . .'

'I'm pissed off with you,' Dee says to Eddie. 'It's extremely bad manners to whisper or to talk behind your hand.' She slaps Eddie's hand. 'Why have you got that thing?' She snatches the mask, which falls on to the floor. After some scuffling she scoops it up and turns it over. 'What is it?'

'Settle down in the back,' warns Orchid Witty.

'Give,' says William.

'I don't think I will, actually, now that you've totally spoilt the evening for me. What is it?' Now Dee turns it over in her hands. 'I shan't give it back unless you tell me what it is.'

'If you can't be quiet I'm going to have to split you up,' says Orchid. Dee puts the gauze into her handbag and snaps it shut.

With Hubert at the helm there had been more to life in PAIN than painting a mural, more than soft toys with the simpering Miss Swift. One winter they had had dancing classes, run by a couple who did a ten-week stint before joining the *QE2*. Sheila had missed the start of the class because she was in the infirmary, so Dee had got a good start without her until the whole shebang was soured by Sheila's return. The whole asylum had danced that winter. On Roma the women had practised their steps and turns between the beds; Sheila had been resting one night while Dee was dancing, practising the Grenadier Two Step, which was full of fast turnabouts. Dee had been dancing and talking, stamping out the rhythm in her black court shoes.

'If I thought it would upset you,' she had said, 'I wouldn't mention it. From what I'd heard, you see, it was all over between you two. If I'd thought anything different then I'd never have considered it. You look a little flushed if I may say so, Sheila. Can I get you a glass or water or something? You do look awfully hot.

'The thing about men, darling, is it's just another need for them. I'm absolutely sure it wasn't anything else. I don't think for a moment it went any deeper than that.' Dee had giggled and clapped her hand across her mouth. 'I mean, God knows, we've known each other for long enough. I am a highly sexed woman, I admit that. And he just threw himself at me, Sheila, and you know what it's like. One minute I was thinking, well, I really hope it's over between them and then the next, well . . . As far I'm concerned it's a one-off. I told him, "We're not making a habit of this, are we, darling?" He knows in any case that I'm already spoken for.

'What I'm saying is, it was waiting to happen. It's been building up for ages, all the time when you were in the infirmary, well, ever since you've been away. You know what it's like, the little hints. Well, of course you know. Working with someone every day, that laundry does get a bit steamed up.' Again the giggle had punctuated. 'So many relationships come about through proximity, we're like animals, darling, give off funny smells.'

Dee had sat herself down on Sheila's bed and begun to rub at Sheila's turned back.

'He's a sweet man, but really, all things considered, rather more your type than mine. All over and forgotten?' She had turned Sheila's hot face towards her and looked into her eyes. 'If I'd thought for a moment that you still held a candle for him, well, nothing would have possessed me . . .' – Dee just hadn't been able to stop herself from giggling – 'particularly when you've had to have this operation and everything.' Dee had rubbed her words into Sheila's back. 'Obviously I was one of the lucky ones and am still, well, very much intact, but I am a woman and I do know what it does to you. It's not simply the knife, is it, sweetie? Thank God they have some counselling these days. It's knowing that you can't ever have a baby, isn't it? That you're not a proper woman any more.'

It had been Orchid, and not Swan's wife Julia, who had supported him through his mother's death; though Julia was on his arm as they entered the church for the funeral it was Orchid on whom his stray thoughts played. Now in these November days the affair with Orchid haunted him. Her admiration, her flattery, had been his lifeline, Swan thought as he drove into the office at the beginning of another week.

The artificial grass that had lined his mother's grave prior to the lowering of the coffin had made Swan think not of Beaker's hairiness but of Orchid's little tapestry cushions: something about the loops of thread. After the burial he had phoned Orchid at once from the double bedroom that his mother had so disliked and later, downstairs at the wake, he had found a way to talk surreptitiously about Orchid.

'She loved sewing,' he had said to an old school friend of his mother's.

'Really? I wouldn't have suspected that.'

'Oh yes,' Swan had lied, thinking of Orchid. 'Always something on the go.'

'Is there anything,' he had asked his sister Margaret, 'that Mum made herself?'

Margaret had looked blank.

'Embroidery or something, sewing?'

'What on earth for?'

'You asked me what I wanted of Mum's. That's what I want. A cushion or something, something she made herself.'

'Sewing? Mum?'

'It's just something Julia mentioned,' Swan had lied. 'I'm sure it's not important. But perhaps you could look and find some little thing... later, when you're going through the clothes.'

'I've done the clothes, Michael, I did that ages ago.'

'So there isn't anything?'

'I don't think so.'

And some weeks later, as the gathering up and enjoying of Orchid had been followed, as it must be, by the setting down, Margaret had brought some bits and pieces over to her brother's and left them in the porch with a note for Julia: 'Is this any good? Do chuck if it's not what you want.' Explaining this little bundle to Julia – two tray cloths and a half-finished tapestry cat with none of the background done (significantly, it now seemed, the words 'Good Luck' still unstitched) – had proved awkward and sewing had not been mentioned again until this particular morning when Swan had unearthed it in the nether regions of the airing cupboard while searching for a missing black silk sock. Looking for a sock is quite enough to unnerve the most robust of men. Swan had been livid, shaking.

'Why can't we get rid of this stuff, Julia?'

'I can't hear you, Michael.'

'Stuffing up the airing cupboard so that one cannot find a single thing!'

'What?'

'Julia!'

'I'm running a bath, for God's sake!'

Swan had stridden into the adjoining bathroom and crossly turned the taps off.

'Michael!'

He had brandished the tapestry cat at her through the steam.

'I said, can't you throw this stuff out?'

'I thought you wanted it?'

'I don't want it!'

'But Margaret said . . .'

'For God's sake, get rid of it!'

'I've grown rather fond of it. I thought I might finish it over Christmas.'

'I don't want it in the house!'

'Well, get rid of it yourself then. Honestly, Michael, I'm trying to have a fucking bath!'

Still in one sock Swan had taken the bundle out to the garbage and stuffed it, as he might stuff Orchid, into the bin.

Now, when he finally got into work in blue socks rather than black – how the ribbing marked his tender calves – he found that Beaker had phoned in sick (a migraine, or in other words, a hangover) and Mrs Eversley from Eventide then rang to say that his father was worrying her; depressed apparently and unhappy, he was talking of taking his own life.

'Where's Orchid?' Swan demanded.

'She's gone to the hawk thingammy . . . sanctuary,' said Paula. 'Mr Baker organized the tickets —'

'What?'

'The portrait painter. He's very good with birds. Orchid says his kestrels are on a par with . . . anyway, she's taken Verne and –'

Taking his own life, an awkward way of putting it, but then Mrs Eversley should feel awkward; after all, it was her responsibility, her fault. Deep in thought Swan left the department so utterly distracted that he took the wrong turn and found himself on the patch of grass that fringed the asylum cemetery. A few Michaelmas daisies, self-seeded, mauve in the forever dusk of the gloomy

November days. Stride purposefully, thought Swan, no doubt you're being watched. His feet were cold. He looked down at them; the grass was wet and he was on it in suede shoes. Walk faster, he thought, do not even think that by the time you get to Eventide he will have done it. Swan would think instead of his conference paper, of single-handedly rekindling an interest in spas. He would think of Preissnitz, after whom they had named a ship.

Swan the pioneer, the conference twinkler. 'Yes, that's right, I hold the line, breaker of new ground, the frontier between sanity and insanity.'

'And the border runs around a marshy lake.'

Orchid should say that, or perhaps the woman he had met at the conference, someone female. Somebody should be in this memorial garden with him this morning but there was no one, only Miller, hidden, watching, from one of the hundreds of identical white, barred windows. My little Gethsemane, thought Swan, getting off the grass and heading back through Hilversum. My little hell, he thought, crossing the Airing Court, circumnavigating the walnut tree and thinking, yes, this morning, for a fraction of a second, I understand why it has been known for inmates to bang their heads against this tree.

'A period of adjustment,' Mrs Eversley was saying. 'So freshly bereaved. Part of a happy family unit here, a community, but your father is, quite obviously, very distressed.'

Swan's sister Margaret was already there, sitting in Mrs Eversley's office with a cup of tea. Swan looked out at the view he was paying for. Above all he felt annoyed. If everybody else settled in, after a period, the period of adjustment ... Hurting his leg at that fire-drill had hardly been a good start. Swan had something on Mrs Eversley, he could sue for that. So. Perhaps his father just needed a little longer than most people to settle. No doubt he was depressed about his leg.

Margaret and Mrs Eversley did the talking and while they talked a vision of Gilbert, an old mate from university, floated into Swan's exhausted brain. Gilbert was his contemporary at college, one of the top brains who had irritated everyone by becoming a Franciscan monk. It was some time since Swan had seen him. Maybe Gilbert was the man to help him through this blip. He would see that Swan was suffering, caring for others and not caring for himself. He ran a community on the east coast; if Swan were to ring him, Gilbert would be understanding, he would be happy to put him up for a few days. But could he go there without Julia? Swan had always pretended to Gilbert that he still loved Julia . . .

Swan's father had threatened to overdose on paracetamol; his son doubted if he had the strength left in him to undo the cap.

'How long has he been in bed?' Swan asked, turning a cold eye on his father lying stubbornly beneath the covers.

'Ten days, twelve . . .'

'Well, he's got to get up. Take an interest. You've got to get up, Dad, you'll make yourself ill.'

Swan's father was unrepentant.

'I want to go home.'

It was cold and Margaret got into the driving seat of Swan's car, forcing her brother to slip into the passenger seat in a move that, in present circumstances, he found uncomfortably symbolic.

'This is your fault,' she said, pressing his car lighter in and taking it out before it was ready, then swearing and doing it again. 'I knew this would happen.' Her cigarette was burning now. Swan pressed the button that opened the electric window.

'I'd like to have him home, Mar, but Julia and I . . . we're both working.'

'Oh, no!'

'I really have an enormous amount on my plate at the moment. Winding things up at work and God knows about the future. I say we let things lie . . .'

'But you know about these things! You know how to cope. She said he was very depressed.'

'Distressed.'

'Well, it amounts to the same thing.' Fresh tears came at the thought of it. 'I couldn't cope, Michael, not with Issy still so little.'

'A child is just what he needs to take his mind off things.'

'Oh, come off it! God, you really take the biscuit, don't you? What am I supposed to do, build an extension?'

'If it's money . . .' Silence in the car, rain dripping off the bloody trees, wet deer. 'I'd pay for it. I mean . . . whatever.'

'If Mummy . . .'

'I can't have him, Mar. It's inconvenient.'

'It *is* inconvenient. Bloody inconvenient! Issy has just started school. I'm fairly free for the first time in years and you turn round and say to me . . . You could have him. Get someone in, couldn't you? A nurse or something, one of your little friends . . .'

'I'm not listening to this, Mar.' Swan got out of the car, apparently fighting for breath, asthma.

Silence.

Brother and sister walked about the car-park, which was deep in fallen leaves.

'It's very pleasant here,' Swan said.

'Obviously not pleasant enough.'

Again silence, broken only by the sound of their feet scuffling.

'Well, will you at least put it to her, talk to Julia?'

Talking to Julia was exactly what Swan couldn't do.

'We'll get it sorted out, won't we?' said Margaret, weakening, calling a truce, taking his arm. 'One way or another. We have to. We must. We can't just leave him somewhere if he isn't happy. It's appalling. We can't do it to him, we must . . .'

Margaret left first. Swan watched her as she put on her seat-belt and then, having trouble getting her hands to her hanky, blew her nose and lit another cigarette. He took the motorway for several miles then swung off and drove on a little way until, looking for somewhere quiet to park, he came upon a small track. A tramp eating a pie sat on a bank, surrounded by a pile of plastic bags. Swan manoeuvred his car so that he couldn't see him and stared ahead instead at a buckled yellow bunker labelled 'Grit'.

Listening to the distant roar of the motorway Swan thought unexpectedly of the small roads that led up to his boarding school and the turn in the drive where in summer you had first sight of boys playing tennis on the courts. Despite or because of his marked intelligence Swan had been unhappy at the school, but his parents had refused to let him leave and to take him home.

His thoughts drifted back to his father. Somewhere . . . closer either to Margaret or himself, some place where Swan could pop in and see the old boy more often. Head round the door, like on a ward round, to jolly things along. Take him out at weekends.

Swan would go and see Gilbert, alone. He needed a break. He started the car, reversed and drove fast through a pot hole, unavoidably splashing the tramp, who seemed to have placed himself deliberately in his path. The tramp shouted after the car, waving his stick. A bundle of brownish rags and the washed-out stripes of someone else's shirt were all too visible in Swan's driving mirror – someone's husband, brother, father, son?

Hubert smoked cigars and wore a duffle-coat and his breath smelt of spearmint to disguise the drink. When the sea froze he visited his mink traps. At weekends he picnicked with the first Mrs Bottril, fishing through the ice. Miller knew and loved the aristocratic voice that talked so knowledgeably about sustenance gained through boiling bones and sucking out the marrow. The smell of spearmint lingered days after the slide show; smelling it was like tasting it himself.

Teapot lid, swimming medal, prescription spectacles . . . Miller, ostracized to the far end of the dormitory because of his restlessness at night and the high smell of his hard yellow feet, lies upon his bed, staring into the semi-darkness, joining up the points made on the lino by the orange lights. Two points of light and his right thigh makes the third point. Miller touches the depression in his leg from an old wound and, as he does so, so he is rewarded, so the thick card that wedges the drawer of his memory becomes dislodged.

Lid, medal and spectacles slide effortlessly to the back of his head, revealing a white sheet of paper written in a firm black hand. Each line on the paper begins with a capital letter and the whole is indented like the depression in his thigh, like a poem. He recognizes the layout before he reads the substance then, as he reads, he feels a pain stir in the wound. Pictures of the pain, triangles that go from sand to ochre. First shock, then pain that leaves him gasping. He can't move, even if he had dared to. He knows he will have to hold on and wait until someone, an expert it would be, comes to his assistance. After the first shock the impact of the pain changes, swinging like a sailing boat gybing. The pain becomes a wheel, wooden and hooped with metal. No sooner has he got used to this new pain than another pain comes, far deeper, a dull pain and a dragging one. The beat of this pain is solemn and relentless. It puts him in his place and keeps him there, suffering and bewildered.

Wrong! Wrong! Wrong! Every pain tells a story and the tale of this pain is truly disconcerting. In pain he sees a god and this god is not what he has expected. Miller has always presumed that he and his god are at the very least contemporaries. They are not. Wrong! Wrong! Everything he has previously taken for granted is wrong. The god he serves is bigger and older than Miller and a great deal more exotic. Miller lies where he has fallen, spread-eagled across three pyramids in Giza, the point of the second pyramid embedded in his leg. Agony seizes his thigh, but the pain in his heart is worse.

Wrong, wrong, diminished! Lying on his bed in Luxembourg he feels again the hot dry wind upon his face and remembers that it was not the god but Hubert Bottril who eventually came to save him. Remembering the pain is hard to bear, but remembering the outcome is even more dismaying, for though Miller was enormous at the time of his fall the god was bigger, and though he had obviously caught sight of Miller he ignored him, simply pointing imperiously at the base of the pyramid, at sand, grains of sand, infinite, brought here by others and piled up in adulation. Sand that hit the eye in the sunlight, crisping the retina, knowledge that really hurt him, for in the bringing of sand lay the seeds of forgiveness and he had dared, presumed, to come here empty-handed.

The chaplain could personally throttle whoever it was who had inserted the word 'Snacks' above his class list. A traffic of inmates flowed in and out of the chaplaincy, leaving the door open, letting out what heat there was from his miserable coal fire. Thank you God, he prays, for imprisoning me in this thorn thicket. Thank you for each rigorous new test. Thank you for the view of the mountain and the knowledge that, should I ever reach the summit, you'll be out.

Unlike his master, David Davies cannot be in two places at once. For security reasons he must leave the church to supervise snacking in the chaplaincy and, as Orchid has observed – this morning she had brought him an enlarged, coloured photocopy of celery and asked him to think about it – precious little painting has been done. Small acts of sabotage, a rat in the sky – it is hard to lay the blame considering the numbers now involved – occur virtually every day.

Those who don't paint but just look on – eating – are equally annoying. William hums monotonously and scribbles in a spiral notebook. Some of the scribbles he tears out and puts into his pocket, others get scrumpled up and chucked into the font. Fatty Barrett insists he cannot paint because his hands are shaky, though the chaplain observes no tell-tale trembling as he lifts a piece of fruitcake to his lips. Fatty Barrett's girth fills the aisle; his bottom, which spreads across two chairs, is cushioned by some kneelers. He coughs fruitcake crumbs and his feet, stuck out in front of him, are an accident waiting to happen. Huddled in his coat he hogs the small gas heater that David Davies pays for out of his own pocket and has felt obliged to bring. Squarely in everybody's way he slumps, oblivious, reading through the sports pages of old newspapers.

William draws in his notebook the oval of a soul and

some little draw-string bags, which he colours in with biro and gives to Eddie for his consideration, labelling them 'blunt gloves'. Humming hard he thinks about the farm. The noises of the farmhouse, the sound of individual bolts and latches, the neck hairs around the collar of the dog as he strains on his leash in the yard. The smell of hawthorn and how its thorns scrape the back of his hand when he dives into it to pull his ball from underneath the hedge. A potent mix of ideas and memory come to him as he sits in the cold chapel and he has hardly time to scribble them down before other ideas come to him and blot them out. Sometimes the sense that he is running after them, can't keep up with them, stops him from doing anything at all.

These days he is more prepared for big hands and other physical surprises. He eats with the others; he still doesn't sleep but the lack of rest no longer bothers him.

High up in his cleaning cupboard William sorts through his pile of dog-ends. Dry tobacco from old roll-ups he sifts into a tin with a piece of orange peel. Rolling a cigarette from the contents he luxuriates for a while before lighting up, timing it for the exact moment that the express train passes the skylight. It is amazing how well he feels. His hands are steady, his head feels clear and light. He puts a steady hand on the crotch of his trousers before taking his trolley down to the psychiatry suite. He feels well, well enough to look out of the window here, to look down at the Airing Court where the others are gathering to wait for their chaperones. How small they look from here. Warren is on duty and he looks small, Eddie looks small, even Miller seems diminished.

Orchid has come in early and William feels a pang of guilt when he sees her, breasts like little pillows.

'You're early this morning, William.'

She is making coffee and stands watching him as he works, as he turns Paula's photo cube round and round and round.

'What are you doing?'

'They all look dense,' says William. 'Some families have really stupid faces, don't they?'

Heading for the lift when his work is done, a small man whom he recognizes calls his attention from a doorway.

'Eh, man. Long time!'

The man reaches up and puts his arm around William's neck, kissing him on both cheeks. He smells strongly of aftershave. He is dressed in the whitest of shirts, his face swarthy and his hair, short in the front and feathered at the back, black against his collar. Now the man stands away from William, appraising him.

'So. How is it with you, eh, William?' He kisses him again, pats his shoulders, shakes his hand. 'William!' he says. 'It's good! Come on, we smoke together, your place.'

So William abandons the trolley and returns with him up the stairs to the cleaning cupboard. He can barely keep up with the man, yet he knows it is imperative to stick with him.

'I'm waiting for you every day. Where you been, eh, William?' He slaps him on the chest. 'Where you been this long time? Hiding from Alfredo? You and me, man, we go back. So how you doing, how's it going with you? All OK with William?' He looks at William as if he can't get enough of him, can't see enough of him, could never see enough. 'You know? I tell you. You gotta problem, you come see Alfredo, right? Never too busy for my friends. Eh, toerag!' he says, chucking his cigarette butt towards the little sink and missing. 'I see you. OK. Give me a call, OK. We talk.

'Hey,' he pauses in the doorway. 'You sort it for me with your sister yet?'

This morning there was an interview with Orchid marked in Swan's diary, arranged through Paula, very formal . . . plus a polaroid of his portrait from the painter clipped to a note suggesting that for a little extra a copy could be made into a fridge magnet. Swan felt a headache coming on.

Julia had spent the weekend in Amsterdam at an exhibition with some girlfriends. It had been a bleak weekend. Dutifully – and it really had felt like duty – Swan had been to Eventide to see his father, bought food and then driven like a mad man to get back home again so that he might start work on his paper. He had tried. Restlessly he had watched television, he had been for a walk – something he never did and in doing so realized why – and had then lain with his feet over the arm of the sofa, plugged into earphones. He had written a letter to a colleague, saying how much he missed the thrill of hands-on psychiatry, bewailing the penalties of high office – all of it a lie. After this he had drunk a brandy in the bath. Swan had opted for consultancy if and when the asylum was wound up but what if he couldn't write the papers he had promised, what if he had really lost his nerve? And what did Orchid want that necessitated such formality? Swan looked from the polaroid to the diary entry. What was the worst scenario he could imagine? Orchid engaged to be married – was that it? This morning he could almost feel the warmth of Hubert's bottom on the chair. What he needed was a good stiff drink.

What would be worse than Orchid marrying? She wanted to take a sabbatical? She was writing a book? A book would be worse than a marriage in Swan's present predicament, in the state he was in over the weekend, barely able to write a single word.

The first thing he had noticed when she had come to see him was the age gap. As she sat across the desk it had never seemed wider, a lifetime stretched between the ages of thirty-two and forty-five. And Orchid was all smiles with that shiny-eyed look of the marathon winner. Orchid had been head-hunted, she was going to leave. She would like to go as soon as possible.

'I imagined you'd want to stay to wind things up?' he had said.

She realized that her 'timing was a bit off' with so many inmate reviews pending, but with his permission she could bring them forward and thus get them done. The job was too good to miss, though obviously its terms and conditions were a bit tight time-wise.

'I pushed them as far as I possible could, Michael.'

'I'm sure you did.'

'You know how tedious it is.'

No he didn't, he had forgotten. Only his head worked, nodded, yes, yes, yes.

Orchid insisted that she had already extended her working day and could get the reviews accomplished in the time left.

'You'll all be seeing rather a lot of me in the next six weeks.'

That would be nice.

'There won't be any loose ends, Michael, I assure you.'

He had wanted to get rid of her, but he did not want her to go.

'Too good an opportunity, of course.' He understood absolutely and they must have lunch some time. The department would have a party for her. She mustn't do anything! They would arrange it all! Swan beamed and stood up to show her from the room, putting his hand out, the paternal hand, the old liver-spotted, feeble, shaky, arthritic, wedding-ringed hand.

'Well done,' he said. 'Congratulations. You always were full of surprises. Funny, when I saw the meeting in the diary I thought you might be writing a book.'

'No time for that, Michael, I'm getting married.'

'Cooee! Vicar!'

The chaplain, caught in the act of prizing the lid off a tin of white emulsion, drops the screwdriver on to the chapel floor.

'Panic not,' Dee says, picking it up for him. 'No, no. Don't even utter! I shan't breathe a word. A desecration. I couldn't agree more. I had an aunt who repeatedly painted the Cob at Lyme Regis. She was the first woman to advertise Yardley's soap.'

Together they look at the mural, now a mess of half-finished paintings superimposed upon each other. Ridout's squat tower is partly obscured, partly revealed by Miller's twisting path that passes through something very much like forest. Two large objects with fanned ends take up the sky.

'The quickest thing always is to question the perpetrator,' Dee says, 'presuming you know who he is. Frankly it looks like a man to me. Always ask, speak up, don't be backward in coming forward. If you don't ask, vicar, you don't get. Oh, but I recognize these,' she says, moving closer to the vicar and the wall to peer at what might be the Egyptian pillars that front PAIN's barrel-vaulted entrance hall. 'I recognize this. This is home!'

'I do have some difficulty . . .' the chaplain says, moving out into the aisle away from Dee. 'Hard to say what any of it is viewed either from a distance or close to. A mural is meant to be read, it's a lesson and I do think this is going to rather muddle some people.'

'What people?'

'People who come here to worship,' he says, eyeing her cigarette.

'But shouldn't they be looking at you, vicar, listening to you? If I had your job I'd insist upon it. It would be rude, surely, unforgivable, to look at the wall. Are you meant to look at the wall during sermons? Do you sing to the wall during a hymn? Those look like God's feet to me.'

A huge sigh escapes the chaplain.

'I think you have a problem with your attitude, vicar. Who is to say that the feet of God are not this size or shape?'

'I don't think God had feet as we know them, Dee,' the chaplain says quietly.

'Sits on my right hand,' Dee says. 'Feet must follow.' Now she too moves out into the aisle and views the mural from a distance. 'Better with the glasses off but definitely six of one and half a dozen of the other, vicar. In so many, many ways muddle is exactly what we want. Provokes discussion, don't you see? Here we are, alone together' – she grinds her cigarette out on a cherub – 'discussing God. And these feet are big enough to be seen from a distance, right from the back of the church. If I believed in God – and excuse me for saying this so bluntly – it would be exactly what I'd want.'

The vicar puts his head in his hands. Dee sits down on the pew next to him.

'We always said our prayers at home, you know, though Nanny wouldn't let us pray for the dogs. And when she'd gone we'd put them in anyway, name after name, a litany of dogs! Binkie, Jacko, Frank, Boy, Jethro, Jake, Bella, Peter and Myrtle. My father was absolutely at one with our local vicar that dogs should not be buried on consecrated ground, but as children we thought it was wrong that they should be at the bottom of creation. I remember in the church, so many of the effigies had their feet on dogs ... Orchid says I really ought to go and see his grave but I'm not having that. Thin end of the wedge. Actually, when Hubert left I thought of him as a dog. People think it's only cats that do it, but dogs can disappear as well. Simply not there one evening when you put their bowls down. I thought that Hubert had run off and would come back again, we all did; as you know it's hard to spot a saint. And none of us who knew him will have any truck with this lot and it's hardly your fault that you represent them, is it? No point getting unduly upset. Orchid asked me just the other day if I wanted to go shopping. I said, "I'll go to the corner with Bullit to post a letter, dear, but that's my lot." "Had I seen the corner?" she said to me. Well, obviously not. According to her there are no corners. "This is a forest," she wittered. "The Royal Mail," I said, "prevails in every corner of the realm." But I ask you, vicar, coming out of university departments, what can they know?

'Personally I don't think we ought to be too concerned about upsetting her, do you? She's got a new boyfriend now, you know. William told me. She can shop with him and get him to buy her pizzas, that's what they eat, food standing up. I've studied it in detail, no wonder they have so many strange ideas. Only animals eat standing up. Cow! OK, I shouldn't say that in the House of God, but I'm sure he'd want me to be honest. No, those are definitely a pair of feet. But what I wanted to talk to you about is nearer to the torso. Knees, vicar. I've been studying the Bible, beetling away, and I've thought of just the thing for kneelers. Maisie can do the sewing, but I'll design them on the theme of "They came to him but he perceived them not." I shall require some squared paper to work it out on and a variety of coloured wools. I should like to them in pinks, mainly, in memory of Sheila Henderson. A selection of vile pinks.'

Alfredo is into women in a big way. Spending time with Alfredo makes William realize how dull Eddie has become. And Alfredo has done well, firing on all cylinders, successful in all departments.

'You wanna start your own sandwich business, William? Eh? Every little thing is possible,' Alfredo says, handling him, touching him, 'but you gotta do things right.'

It is good to have someone helping him. Together they get through the cleaning at a cracking pace, but Alfredo is critical of many of William's ways and particularly of his appearance.

'No, no,' he says. 'This is nowhere, man, OK?' He stands next to William, looking at him in the mirror on the inside door of the cleaning cupboard. 'You wanna get a woman, then you listen up Alfredo well, eh? You listen how Alfredo makes his hair. Good hair. Conditioned hair. You know you don't get good hair like this, but like this.' He wets William's hair, making it lie flat. 'You wanna lady so you gotta look good, like Alfredo look good. So you smarten up, eh? Percentage of your time, William. Now tell me you understand. So many per cent on cleaning, so many on the mirror. See, you got it. You learn quick. You and me we work together, we get results. See that Eddie? He's going no place, no place! You stick with me, eh? Looking good. 'I show you good way with machine. OK. So some day you don't bother getting it out, OK? Why go over carpet is already fine? Stupid, eh? You spend percentage making yourself look good. You must get time from somewhere, time is not grow on trees, William.

'Waste paper in the bag,' he says, emptying the basket into the bin bag and missing the opening. Paper spills out everywhere, Paula's tissues go all over the floor. 'Quick!'

This morning there is hardly any paper in the bag, but they take it down in the lift together. When Alfredo closes the lift door William feels uneasy. He tries to raise his hand to press 'G' for ground, but his hand is full of water and he cannot lift it from his side. Alfredo is oblivious, lying on the floor of the lift with his hands behind his head, sunbathing.

'All my life,' he says, 'is the Virgin. I go to her, I lie in front, she says, "Make yourself look good, Alfredo. I speak to Jesus, he likes pretty boys."'

William tries again to raise his hand to the lift button. He is right by the button but his hand won't work. He can't press it, so he pushes himself against it; he doesn't want to be stuck in the lift.

'You don't tell Alfredo shut up, OK?' Alfredo says, though William has said nothing. Alfredo jabs the button with his finger then points the finger at William's head as if it were a gun. The lift descends, the door opens. Alfredo backs out with the trolley then stops, the trolley half in and half out of the door. William steps back until he can feel the steel wall of the lift against his shoulders. Alfredo pushes the trolley back into the lift so that it touches William's toes.

'Alfredo here to help you looking good,' he says. 'So how you get this woman? You get her alone. You say, "After class, carry your bag." Eh? That's the way it is and always is. She smell like shit, you say she smell like rose. Then you get it. What you want.'

If he had time William would work out his percentage, would look from Eddie to Alfredo, from Alfredo to Eddie. But there is no time and Alfredo is impatient for a decision.

'Sleep is for sissies,' Alfredo says as William watches Eddie sleeping. His shore, his lifebelt, his safety, his stone. In the darkness of a winter dawn William sits on the edge of his bed and writes a note to Eddie. 'I know if I was going I'd appreciate the gloves.'

Eddie has burnt his hand on the iron and the bandaged hand – poor wounded hand – lies on top of the covers, the bandage partly unravelled. William leans and touches Eddie, fingers to fingers.

'Getting your attention,' Alfredo says bitterly. 'My poor hand, my fucking flat feet! I don't think you fall for that. We looking after ourselves here, don't you know? You care nothing for me, nothing! So goodbye, eh, William? Because your friend Alfredo is not treated as a friend. Alfredo now is leaving!'

'I need help,' says William.

'You need boys, I get you boys. Plenty boys. Nice boys. Then you say it's women. Tell and I get it for you, what you want.'

Solace is the laundry, solace is Eddie, solace is being in the bakery alone.

'Is fucking drag music!' Alfredo says with malice, fiddling with the knob of the bakery's transistor radio. He moves the channels so that they are nowhere, in the middle of something, fuzzy.

'Listen up,' he says to William. 'That's your head!'

These dank November days William meets Alfredo round every corner. He even meets him in the bogs. And the moment Alfredo sees him Alfredo starts talking.

'Ask her pull you a pint,' he says in the canteen, and

when William turns to take his tea back to the table, there is no place for him. Alfredo is sitting with Eddie. This is hell, yet strangely in this hell William, standing up by the counter, can see heaven: a summer of drought, but the sheep are shorn and their year-old lambs lie under the shade of the ilex. The leaves are grey and plentiful and the flocks are vast yet lie silent, settled in small groups under the holm-oaks on the dusty grass.

Forced by Dobie to share a table with Miller, William watches his friends, watches with amazement as Alfredo takes Eddie's book, careful to mark the page, and closes it. Then he serves Eddie, bringing him a plate of cereal and toast with another side plate over it, whisking a napkin on to his lap.

At William's table Miller shovels porridge into his mouth, slipping the goo between the brown stumps of his teeth. His tabard is too short for him and, unlaced, the tough reflective plastic meets the edge of the table like a baby's rigid bib. Fatty Barrett tries to sit at Eddie's table and Alfredo politely offers up his own chair.

'Nah. No worries,' Fatty Barrett says. 'I can see you two have business.'

And they have. As William watches he sees Eddie take a note out of his pocket and smooth it out on the table. It is William's note. Eddie slides it across the table to his new companion. Alfredo glances at it then spreads his hands in a wide gesture of disbelief. He shakes his head as if to say, It's hopeless, and Eddie gives a knowing smile as plum jam oozes off Miller's toast and runs on to the tabard-bib.

'Watching a train you never gonna catch!' Alfredo sneers, pulling William roughly away from the skylight in the cleaning cupboard, tipping up the bucket that he

113

is standing on.

'You wanna see something, then you come along with me. Hey!' he says. 'Hold up a minute. Bin bag!'

William takes a bag from the drawer.

'Give it! Give!' Alfredo licks the top of the bag so that it opens easily, big and wide. Then he leans into the cleaning cupboard, fingering William's hidden treasures, settling on the pottery head of a baby and deliberately allowing it to slip out of his hands so that it smashes half in the basin, half on to the floor.

'Baby, please don't go!' Alfredo sings, the pointed toe of his shoe among the pieces.

'Wait! Please!' calls William, struggling with the slithers of pottery on the floor and in the basin, shoving them through the black lips of the bag.

'Morning, morning.' Dr Swan is looking remarkably dapper in his suit among the overalls and tabards and the grime of the old buildings. He floats above it all, a picture of serenity. He pats old Prennely on the back.

'Difficult for everybody,' he says.

'It's going ahead then, sir? Just that the others have been . . .'

'It's going to go smoothly, Prennely, over the next couple of months. I'm relying on you to set the tone, you know.'

'Thank you, sir.'

'Part of the old brigade.'

'Thank you, sir.'

This is as much conversation as Prennely expects, as he has a right to expect. The doctor is a busy man and yet he lingers.

'Everything all right at home? Mrs Prennely? Good,

good. One thing I did want to mention, and I certainly wouldn't want you to take this personally Prennely, but in the modern world . . . I want you to know that I have let it be known that there is no way, Prennely, I mean no way, that we could dispense with your services through voluntary redundancy, so I have suggested that your nephew . . .?'

'Warren.'

'Exactly.'

Prennely pales. Swan continues rapidly.

'Now tell me. How do you think he'll take it? Think he'll be all right? The point is . . . that his training . . . that I know that you have given . . . provided him with . . . will stand him in good stead whatever he does but I'd like to know, I should like you to come and let me know, what his plans are for the future. I wouldn't like you or your . . . ?'

'Sister?'

'Exactly . . . to think we have wasted your time. Discipline, wouldn't you say, is what these boys so badly need. I thought so, and in that department I'm sure that you have —'

'He wants to go travelling, sir.'

'Oh — really?'

'Eastern Europe.'

'Well, that's very . . . admirable.'

Prennely and Swan have walked around the Airing Court. Both hesitate before taking a second circuit round the tree.

'Very enterprising these days, wouldn't you say, Prennely? These young people. Everything's changed, of course . . .' Swan heads for the long bench placed against the wall of Roma. 'No, no. Come on, sit down, time we had a proper chat. Yes, it's really changed. Hard to believe really that this old place . . .'

'Very fond of it in my own way,' says Prennely.

'Absolutely.'

'They don't know it like we do,' Prennely ventures.

'Yes,' says Swan doubtfully. 'That's probably it.' Now that the two are sitting down a wheel drops off the conversation; it bumps along, it trundles.

'I suppose I'd better, we'd both better be getting on. Anyway, Prennely, I'm glad we've had the chance to have a little talk. And do pass on my good wishes to . . .'

'Warren.'

'Won't you. Wish him all the best.'

'Readiness.' Orchid knows it upside down and inside out, she knows it in her bones, along her hairline, she knows it in the tingle of her fingertips. Orchid knows what to look for and when she has found it she will defend her decision at the clinical meeting before the papers can be signed. Queen of the review board, who decides when inmates are ripe to be released. Is it a science she practises or is there an X-factor, an intuitive response to inmates, a certain something, a reading between crossed lines?

William waits to see her in the foyer. He is the first of this morning's appointments and he is smartly dressed. Though he is not here to work she watches from her office as he feeds the fish. Opening and closing her mini-secateurs – cut right back, her motto for the potted plant – she watches William's lips move as he scatters food on to the surface of the water. She must put him at his ease first. She joins him in the foyer.

'A glass of water, William?'

He would like to do it for her, but he does not trust his hands.

'Well,' she says, shepherding him into her sanctum, seating him next to her on the little sofa. 'I expect you miss the country at this time of year, William?'

He says he does; does she know that he doesn't? Know that what he misses every morning is the time before Alfredo: up in his own room with a pilfered cigarette, that glimpse of the express train.

He has changed his hairstyle and his shirt is neatly tucked into his trousers. The tabard, for so long simply slung on, is now fastened securely at both sides.

'Make yourself comfortable, William.'

'Over in no time, mate,' Alfredo says.

William mutters something in reply.

'Sorry?' says Orchid.

'Nothing. Just clearing my throat.'

Inmates are understandably nervous; after all, there is a grapevine in here, they know exactly what is at stake. Once the process has begun, its progress is inexorable. Decisions are acted upon and cannot be reversed. A special demeanour is required of the acting officer. While she listens she assesses every nuance, every little thing that will bolster her theory of readiness. Behaviour patterns, relationships with other people, she has got it all on file. She smooths her little skirt and puts a hand down the fine Lycra of her tights. There will be plenty of eye contact during this meeting; for the moment she is content to see her own reflection in those patent shoes.

Orchid will take her patient down and there is nothing like that shot of adrenalin that forwards a case history, that empties a bed – O mighty Queen who draws that thick line through a file! Down, down, deep down, Orchid will take you down to a place by the water, quite confident that she knows you better than you know yourself. You stand on the edge with Orchid and hold her hand, this is the zenith of your sojourn in the institution. At this point you receive her total attention: you are the one and only one in whom she is interested, you are special to her, extra special, such attention from the sun is overwhelming, you imagine affection, fondness, love ... for what Dr Beaker the Squeaker deconstructs Orchid chooses now to reassemble. Here in this green room the bits and pieces that you were before you came inside may be given back to you if you can prove – as she wants you to prove, as she hopes you will prove – that you are strong enough to shoulder them again. Relationships from the other world, children, parents, siblings, spouses; and could you cope on rent day? Can you fill a form in? Would you find a job?

The bits and pieces that jangled for precedence so that you felt like screaming and you did scream. That churned in your stomach until your stomach was something that was sick. That pulsed through your veins, that once visualized became obsessive, so that the very sound of your own circulation was deafening. The awful pump that spread the poison round your body, the liquid that swirled in your abdomen and went up and down your legs, that spurted from your arms when you cut them, that sung in your ears so that silence was something you could not even distantly recall. All that poisonous noise that Beaker siphoned out of you, that spilt across his desk and stained his carpet long ago, can Orchid be confident that the mess you once were has been thoroughly cleaned up?

Orchid has got the lot if you are interested, reconstituted, repackaged in see-through plastic bags for you to look at. And you can have it all back now if your attitude is right. Look at the bags of your life that Orchid holds in front of you and prove to her that you really want them, that you satisfy – as she sincerely hopes you will – the check-list of convictions you will need so that you may be restored to the world beyond these walls. Years that you thought meant nothing, time that seemed suspended to no point, but everyone's been watching you, everyone and all the time. Everyone has sent reports, now that she has deigned to ask for them; all that is needed now is for her to hear it from the horse's mouth.

William sits on the sofa in this green room with Orchid, hair bobbed, legs crossed, a vision framed by plants with freshly misted glistening leaves. One to one, or so she thinks, for Orchid has never met Alfredo, is unaware that he exists. Blissfully oblivious, this little mite in bright red tights and patent shoes, completely unaware of how Alfredo has tutored William so that he knows now how to play it, to enthuse a little, not too much. Just enough so that his attitude remains above suspicion because, because . . . because isn't it something else, something altogether other that our William really wants? Something secret that Orchid must not know? Alfredo is man of vast experience; he knows that it is when you are feeling better that you find you have the energy and the courage to consider it. It is now, now, not at the beginning of the file that in preparation for this review board Orchid has perused.

The beginning is where Orchid starts with William, early days when his will was as weak as the cabbage soup served in the Russian Sergeants' School. The beginning when William arrived here, when he was fed and doped and watered, exercised, returned to bed – does Orchid know that William thought about it even then? Thought about it with longing, dreamt about it, dwelt upon it, almost physically luxuriated in it? Yes, she probably suspects. The insurance policy he treasured, does she know he kept those payments up? It isn't Eddie but Alfredo who is William's stalwart guardian, Alfredo who has run him through all possible versions of this interview. Teaching William that he must do nothing now that could be misinterpreted, misinterpreted by those who have different ideas for his future, what is fitting, what is right. What is what. What is acceptable, what is sane. If the dead could talk they would mention an Alfredo who came in the last few weeks to teach them how to go.

Orchid, Orchid, breasts like little pillows near enough to stretch towards and touch. How can you bear to disappoint her now? Orchid who takes you down to the water when she considers you are ready to go in. This is the moment at which yielding is a possibility, because it is easier, so much easier, when someone is rough with you, easier if you had a Dobie, not a sweet Orchid, on your case. Easier than this beguiling listening. You have to watch your expression when you speak to her, she reads your thoughts or she thinks she does. You wouldn't want her to catch you looking gleeful when she spoke of death.

She looks radiant today but William mustn't touch her. Any sudden movement will frighten her off. William sits awkwardly, hands clenched inside his pockets. Show willing and she will take you down and it is all much more beguiling than William had anticipated.

'I expect you miss the country, William?'

She will take him there. Now it is William but it might be you who sees the water glint between the trees. You follow her in single file, for the way is narrow and there is only room for one. Ferns have grown up since you were last there. She pushes them aside with her hand and they sway back and forth , back and forth. The bay is just big enough for you two to stand together. Someone has had a fire here and you think, Yes, that's right, or even, I remember. There are midges in the evening, a fire in a circle of stones and a log for Orchid to sit upon.

The ground slopes gently towards the water and it is moist and damp. You and Orchid are the first humans here this morning, your footprints on the bank like the first marks in snow. The most gentle summer breeze ruffles the surface of the lake, the tiniest of ripples wetting the small, smooth, muddy stones. Too small, too ordinary – be careful, William – to mark the frontier between the water and the land?

Orchid takes William by the hand and he stands with his toes just in the water, which is cool and beautiful. At the edge of the lake – in the silence he can hear it – each time the water ripples, there is the very faintest, faintest sigh followed by the very faintest suck. Suck, sigh, as easy as breathing in and out. And Orchid says that he may go in if he wants, test the water, breast-stroke out into the water, swim.

The surface of the lake is warmer than its depths. William finds a gentle stroke that keeps him near the surface so that he can avoid the cold. And oh! the water is delicious. He turns on his back and floats, lily pads, dragonflies ... he ducks down and comes up with his hair streaming, ducks down but makes sure he comes up again. Don't stay under too long, warns Alfredo, or Orchid may have to buzz.

She doesn't want to buzz, she wants to free you, she much prefers to listen to what she expects to hear. She listens intently just to William, head very slightly cocked, without once looking at the clock. She knows – the university degree – how long three-quarters of an hour is and she will begin to wind her patient down minutes before the end, just before his chaperone turns up.

Once William has gone Orchid hunches and opens her shoulders, relaxing the muscles that have been strained by this intense listening. She does a set of yoga exercises, standing up and stretching up her arms. Her hands reach up to touch the computer-coloured photos of the brain sliced in section that have become far too familiar for her to see. Inmates are often late for their appointments; the business of this institution is waiting, hold-ups, cock-ups . . . in the interim she looks into the side pocket of her briefcase and feels for a pack of newly developed photographs. Orchid and the portrait painter on their visit to the Hawk sanctuary. The painter with his field glasses, Orchid with the flask.

'She won't push me around,' Dee says to Maisie when William enters the Airing Court. 'I'm not having it. It's not on. I'm so on edge, I just can't tell you. Last night I hardly got a wink! Then she says she's worried about me – not that word, the other word, Maisie, the word I hate . . . "Concerned", as if I were any concern of hers? She said that if I wished to sleep in the day then it was quite all right for me to go back up to the dormitory. So insulting all of it, treating me as if I couldn't stick the pace.'

Dee will Superglue herself to the scuffed skirting boards if they try to move her, or she thinks she will. She will cradle the moth-eaten fire blanket, she will run screaming down the corridor and into a dark corner with her perished hot-water bottle and her favourite broken cup. 'Move it and you'll have to move me!' she will cry, her back against a cupboard that is too warped to shut.

'I shall enter the mode of direct action, Maisie, and I am not joking about this. They'll have to hoick me screaming from the gas brackets, they'll have to break my fingers and my toes.'

The gable clock chimes the quarter. Dee and Eddie to the laundry, William to the bakery; Alfredo stands before him on the path. He says he wants the cleaning cupboard and that William must help shift his treasures to another place.

122

'No baking today,' Alfredo says. 'You come along with me.'

William would do it properly if Alfredo would stop hassling him. As it is his hands shake as he takes his treasures from the shelf. Three Walkmans, a bar of buttermilk and clover soap, a clothes brush with a rotatable head, an eighth of dope, a small square of chamois leather sewn around a piece of wood as a nail buffer, a postcard of Isambard Kingdom Brunel, a turquoise earring (probably Miss Swift's), a little cone-shaped pewter cup that could be a dice shaker or part of a hip-flask set, some writing he did when he first came in here. All of it must be gathered up – quickly! – into a bag.

Where are they going? Alfredo isn't telling. Wherever it is it is far beyond the reach of CCTV. Weaving to the left, to the right, squeezing behind a sheet of corrugated iron, left again and round the corner, into the echoing emptiness of abandoned Finisterre.

There are no lifts in here and William is puffing by the time he reaches the first floor. Bed heads, mattresses, pillows, paper, dust and daddy-long-legs dangling from the cobwebs. Though the layout is exactly the same as Hilversum, Luxembourg and Roma, William is disorientated in here. All is gloomy and brooding in the half-light, echoing to the sound of his heartbeat as he holds on to the banisters for breath.

Alfredo goes ahead with the bag of treasures, pieces of which tumble out and down the stairs, shouting at William, 'Eh? You coming or what?' From the landing William looks down a corridor truncated with rubbish of all sorts. His eye sticks in that corridor. At his feet is a tangle of a coat hangers. 'Eh, man!' William turns to the second flight of stairs and his eye sticks again, this time to the wall. Here and, when he looks, yes, there at the rail of the banister, the pillar that supports the stairs, the door frames in the corridor, all are alive with etched graffiti. Words are scratched on to the metal window bars, on to the bed heads; initials, drawings, whole messages. APW PFD GAW, hearts and then an anchor and more initials. Everywhere he looks, there is this instinct towards identity, remember me? And William knows in his heart and in his head that it is a mistake to linger, that it is dangerous to look and he hears the sharp click of Alfredo's Cuban heels.

Alfredo has ditched the bag somewhere and has caught William looking at the walls for, despite his best instincts, William finds he cannot tear his gaze away. And now Alfredo takes his hand and pulls at his fingers, making him trace the initials that have been gouged into the tongue-and-groove boarding, into the plaster, into the brick. Making him put his finger right down and in and feel the letters. It feels to William as if his finger has passed through flesh and into bone.

William knows what he didn't want to know, he knows it absolutely. The past is not past, it waits to pounce upon the future, the way the bastard of a cat pounces. As he closes his eyes to shield himself so he hears the calling, all of them calling, identifying themselves through their initials, wind in the sounds of 'William!', quicksand in the dreaded words 'Remember me'.

In Finisterre the rooms are full, not empty. People in cots, in chairs, on benches, lying crossways on the unmade beds. Cord around the neck of one man who wears a metal number, 121, cords around the necks of child-like adults tagged like dairy cows. William stands in the shadow of the doorway where they can't see him until, unable to resist, he is drawn into the room. Silence for a moment and then the chatter starts again, cold hands, cold feet, dry furred tongues, the smell of their breath, the sound of their shallow respiration. A woman in a checked overall, the sleeves rolled, the hands clasped, the forehead wrinkled and the corners of her mouth inclining down; and here another, shoulders rigid, body stooped. Voices mutter to each other, sorrow, sadness, morbid apprehensions. He traces the word chiselled into the windowsill. 'Remember me!'

One bites her knuckles before pointing out to him a network of elliptical lines that run along the floor and up the wall, tracing the last rays of the sun; another passes him, leaving an after-smell of secretions and sweat. He is called across the room by a smiling girl with a handkerchief in each hand, beside her the pink bodies of hairless mice crawl over one another in a nest made in the centre of a mattress and Alfredo says William must count the number of the mice and not forget the number. Further into the room the tone of the chatter changes into something seething, irritable, restless. A woman in a full-length gown, grey hair to her waist and a hand on her hip, hollers into nothing.

So they distinguish themselves, so William drinks them in. Around and about him, the bird-like faces of microphalics quarrelling by a little corner sink; the dry-skinned, dwarfish, stumpy hands and feet of Mongolian syphilitics and cretins; a woman labelled 'Wastrel', prostitutes and inebriates stripped down to the waist; and here a catatonic with his jacket buttoned, fists clenched, eyes closed, arms held out before him. Three to a cot in the corner and against the wall, sitting on each other's knees, they topple from the stacks of metal chairs. Deaf mutes gather to listen, catatonics hold their poses for the photograph to be invented, melancholics pose, backs turned to a picture of a Harvest Home they cannot see. On and on through all the rooms of Finisterre goes William, to where syphilitics,

sitting in a perfect circle, pick each other's sores and a
cretin with apples in her apron leans against a bathroom
door. A silent group in dressing-gowns shiver at the turn of
the staircase, listening to the splash of water. The raucous
chorus of initials sings 'Remember me!'

Alfredo cruises through, but William is caught by the
shirt tails, by the straps of his tabard, by the laces of his
shoes, by the hair on the back of his neck. He walks as if
through heavy water. At the very top of the staircase is a
series of maids' rooms. The shadows of numbers long
fallen away mark each door. They enter number 8. There
are two narrow beds and a skylight like the one in the
cleaning cupboard. On the wall is a square of darker wallpaper where a looking-glass once hung and Alfredo tells
William to look into it and do his hair. 'Eh! William,
smarten up!' Faded sweet pea wallpaper peels in strips
from the wall and Alfredo takes a ticking pillow and empties William's bag of treasure close to it. He makes William
arrange his things like the crown jewels but William has
never seen them and he cannot do it right. So he lays them
out again and again until, with little adjustments, Alfredo
is satisfied: the dope, the square of chamois leather, the
earring, the soap, the clothes brush, the postcard, two
Parker pens and one Schaefer that he had quite forgotten
and three Walkmans, one of which is taped up with the
name of the owner written on to the masking tape.

'Kneel!' Alfredo says, and William tries to kneel in the
space between the iron beds.

'Your hair is wrong. Are you ashamed of it?'

'Yes.'

'Louder!'

'Yes.'

'So brush your hair with a hedgehog and don't turn
round!'

126

It is hard not to turn when he is pulled towards the bedroom doorway, faces peering in at him, witnessing his humiliation.

'I do it!' Alfredo says and brushes William's hair until the scalp bleeds. 'Are you ready now?'

'Yes,' says William, though he cannot know for what he is meant to be ready. Alfredo stands above and behind him on the bed, placing William's hands over his eyes, then knees him in the back to wind him.

'Say you are not clean!' Alfredo insists.

'I am not clean.'

'So?'

'So?'

'I am not clean so I must eat the soap.'

A cold wind cuts through the Airing Court. Inmates stamp their feet upon the asphalt and tuck their hands under their armpits to keep warm.

'"Within the woody pass,"' quotes Eddie, '"... at a level anything lower than the horizon, all was dark as the grave. The copse wood . . . the copse wood . . . a dog barked and it's only a pause in the barking . . ."'

'Verne's been out and he says it was terrible,' barks Dee to Eddie. 'Strapped into that dreadful car and she refused to put the seat back and it was agony on his neck. And the traffic! He said his ears were ringing for at least three days. And she was going on and on, of course, as per. Empty vessels, Eddie, mark my words.'

'Where's William?'

'Don't interrupt me when I'm talking, Eddie.'

'Have you seen him this morning?'

'Well, I saw him but he didn't see me.'

'"Within the woody pass . . ."'

'Anyway, as I was saying, she went on and bloody on. Wouldn't he like to choose his own deodorant and did he want a pair of socks? She had money, she said, and he had only to point at what he wanted.'

'Why are we waiting?' chants Fatty Barrett, taking a jump at Miller and tipping off his fez.

'Chuck it, Barrett!' Ridout calls but the throw is short and the hat lands at Dee's feet.

'Take that *thing* away from me!'

'Kick it here!' shouts Ridout.

'I certainly shall not.'

Fatty Barrett scoops it up and kicks it high in the air and into the bare branches of the walnut tree.

William keeps his eyes closed until he is sure Alfredo has gone. Opening his eyes at last he focuses upon the treasures on the floor. He picks up the little square of chamois leather and thinks not of goats but of the warm flanks of cows and the thwack heard two fields away, that slap to get them moving, and the holler of the cowman calling them up through the early morning misty fields. Somewhere in this pile there must be photographs; pictures of him in the boiler suit that stank of silage, photographs of him with the dog in the yard. He hears the holler of the cowman then the pumping in the parlour, but he cannot see himself. Not in the dairy or in the yard or in the farmhouse. Where is he if not by the river in the city, if not in the valley below the downs? The call comes again and the only places that William sees himself, his height marking him out in every picture, are in the canteen, in the dormitory on Luxembourg, in the Airing Court, in the soft-toy class, in the Wet Weather Room, and the call comes, urging him to another place he doesn't want to be. The holler is occasional but insistent. William lies on the bed listening until he can bear it no longer and turns on his elbow. He sees again the faces at the door.

'You're not yellow, are you, William?'

Yes, he has been yellow all his life and he has never been quick and he can't think under pressure; how they press for a decision, those faces at the door.

A small woman detaches herself from all the others, apples gathered in the corners of her long grey apron, a dark face framed by the ties of her white cap, and here at last is a photograph he is pleased with. Pencil marks on the airing cupboard in the farm's big cold bathroom, marks of a 'W' and the dates written next to them.

'William, look how tall you've grown!'

'Count to ten,' the little woman says to William, showing him the quick way down.

Part 2

RELIEF for Swan would be to talk of something else or not to talk at all. To have fewer cups of coffee made for him and particularly not to have to touch people, to pat them on the back, on the shoulder, on the arm, to pat Orchid on the arm and not on the bottom. Not to be forced to proffer consolation on a plate with platitudes. 'Look. With the best will in the world . . .' Not to feel the softness as he touches Orchid, not to want to touch her somewhere else. And not to have to deal with everything, to take responsibility that in truth just makes him want to sink his head in Orchid's skirt. And, believe it or not, among the vast recesses of the Swan medical cabinet there is nothing for a sore throat.

'Eye patch, support stocking, finger-stall . . .' Swan shouts accusingly.

'Well, take an aspirin.'

'Haven't you got one of those lemony things?'

'No, I haven't!'

It is obvious that Julia doesn't care about his throat.

'I can't look at the fish but I see him feeding them,' Paula says. Swan, of course, could never look at the fish.

Up to him, is it, to arrange the department and anyone else who feels like mourning all around the fish tank for some finny reassurance? Now there is going to have to be an inquiry and tedious meetings and an interview with Prennely; how he will love it, the shortcomings of CCTV. So this is the ultimate in the blip stakes and Swan has got a terrible sore throat.

On the morning of William's memorial service Swan plans to get in early. More blips as he finds himself in a traffic jam less than a mile from the house. A tree has fallen in the road and he is stuck behind it. Naturally the road is narrow. A few motorists do U-turns. Swan gets out of his car and immediately regrets it, surrounded by a chirping of early morning birds keen to stick their beaks in:

'So sorry to read about your trouble.'

'I suppose it's almost inevitable? Law of averages.'

'How *do* these things happen?'

'Nasty business, if you ask me.'

Swan has such a sore throat he can barely squeak. What he would like to do is hire a plane that flew a streamer reading 'Yes, I am ultimately responsible. Now for Christ's sake leave me be!'

The tree has clipped the roof of a pair of terraced cottages, bringing down the wires.

'Be careful what you touch,' warns someone. 'We don't want anyone electrocuting themselves just before Christmas.'

Beyond the motorists a large woman in a quilted nylon jacket and headscarf, cabriolet legs licked about by Labradors, has started slicing through the trunk of the tree with a chain saw. Her husband appears at the door of the cottage, bearing cups of tea. The road is wet and their breath stands in the cold air, dense with the sweet smell of fresh sawdust.

'If we form a chain we can get this done fairly quickly.'
A wet log is passed into Swan's hands.

'Frontier spirit!' screeches the woman in the headscarf.

'Come on, then,' says a van driver, his jacket pocket displaying the logo of a hatchet and the words 'Crazy Prices We Cut Everything'. ' Come on,' he says. 'From you to me.'

Just in time. Dr Beaker, stuffed into a black suit, turns as Swan tiptoes up the aisle of the chapel and makes room for Swan on the pew.

'I am the resurrection and the life, saith the Lord: he that believeth in me, though he were dead . . .'

'We don't want to listen to this, do we, Bullit?' Dee is heard to say. 'We don't want to be noticed or included. We'll look to our own salvation, thank you very much.'

'We are gathered here together this morning to remember William Carter, our brother in Christ. Will you please all stand for the first hymn.'

A piece of cloth has been hung over the mural and Beaker points it out to Swan. David Davies notices Beaker pointing; how he wishes now he had been more generous with the snacks. Looking down through his church he sees the font, so recently full of William's bits of scrumpled paper.

> When the solemn death bell tolls
> For our own departed souls,
> when our final doom is near,
> Jesu, son of Mary, hear.

Why was it Miller he had given the sweets to, not William? Why was it that there was nothing he could do and say this morning to compensate for the waste of

135

William? Youth, the word haunted him, the tender age of the young man.

When the heart is sad within
With the thought of all its sin,
When the spirit shrinks with fear,
Jesu, son of Mary hear.

'I wonder you didn't see it coming,' Dee says, grabbing the opportunity to talk through the singing. 'But then you do have a blind spot, don't you, Eddie? First Sheila and now William . . . Maisie said that being close to you was like being close to the Grim Reaper, but I don't think that's fair. It's not your fault that you're completely and utterly oblivious. How can you notice anything when your head is always in a book?'

'We will now kneel for a moment in silent prayer.'

'Count me out!' says Dee.

Eddie is the rock that William sheltered under; the only thing safer than Eddie was death. Now Eddie puts his face into his hands. Beside him Miller mutters, but he isn't praying.

'Within the woods,' Miller says remarkably, 'all was dark as the grave.'

The crackle of a radio diverts them all, a voice from the gatehouse asking for clearance for the van from Crazy Prices.

'For pity's sake!' says Dee as Dobie takes the radio outside.

'The grace of our Lord Jesus Christ, and the love of God, and the fellowship . . .'

'We'll all be punished,' Dee says as the inmates wait in the chapel for their chaperones. 'They'll round us up,

Eddie, mark my words, it's only a matter of time. Bullit knows when he's going to the kennels, don't you, pet?'

Mrs Brande is recovering from flu. Just thirty-six hours ago she lay on a pitching bed dreaming that she was foreign correspondent in St Petersburg. Now, thank God, the bold stripe in her wallpaper no longer converges or expands and her appetite is restored – she has been downstairs twice for toast and tea.

Though weakened she is once more the canteen manager of PAIN, responsible for missing teaspoons and for stacking powdered soup mixes. Sensibly she stays in bed to convalesce, listening to a radio short story, 'Kynance, It Was Kynance', set in a rugged cove. The ordeal of paracetamol and wet flannels and over-diluted fruit squashes is over, but relief is laced with resentment at missing everything on television and not being in full control of the downstairs of the house. Christopher has, of course, done nothing, Mr B. has done his best but this will not be good enough . . . a wave of depression floods the cove and her eyes well with tears that are general: shock and sadness over the death of William Carter rolls like a snowball, picking up the sundry miseries that afflict her life. The world of work and particularly the treatment of Miller that, though she has never breathed a word, upsets her; the relationship with Frank Prennely that never achieved lift-off, the anxieties about Christopher, the hideous thought of Christmas, the fact that her hair needs streaking – how it hurts when they pull it through that rubber cap – and Mr Brande won't notice anyway; the lack of oomph in Mr Brande. Yes, it's him who is to blame for all of it and for some reason this morning it has finally got to her, the crunch, the nub, that the Brandes will never now buy that caravan.

In a couple of days she will be back at the asylum, her responsibilities as heavy as the coat she will have to put on to wait for her bus in the rain. Mrs Brande considers winter and this in turn reminds her of her best friend at school, who emigrated to Australia on the one-pound ticket. Trying not to see the piles of newspapers, the general mess of the downstairs of her house, Mrs Brande gathers what she needs and tucks herself back up in bed, props herself on the pillows and writes to Veronica Moran.

Dear Veronica

I am sorry not to have written for so long but have been very busy at work. I suppose this must be your summertime? You are not missing much here. It's dark when I go to work and dark when I get back, it's been the wettest and windiest November since 1981 when we had snow. Mr B. and I are going to take a week at Easter and go to Kynance Cove again. We always have really good sex there and it's not true, as you well know, that it all stops when you're menopausal. An old friend of mine is very ill and I fear it may be his last confusion. He escaped in 1981 and, though he broke his leg in two places, got as far as the north coast. I must alert the authorities that this wet weather may conspire to bring it all up again.

Yours in haste,

Doreen Brande

PS It is my opinion that inmates should be permitted to have pets.

Is that PS all right? Doreen deliberates before sealing the letter, knowing all the while that she won't send it. She has no address for Veronica, never has had.

When Doreen returns to work she takes Christopher in with her. The death of William has undermined her confidence completely. She must keep an eye on Christopher, protect him from evil, place her bulk between him and temptation.

'It's people going in and out of your life at this age,' she says to Prennely, but Prennely is preoccupied.

'An apple Danish, if you will, Doreen.'

Cakes and pastries. It had been one of the small pleasures of her working life, a very small one, to arrange them nicely in the glass cabinet. Now Orchid says that cakes will have to go. A pack of yellow forms issued by Orchid sits underneath the lip of Doreen's counter. No extra pay, of course. Orchid wants Doreen to take a note of what is eaten and by whom.

'I think you'll be able to follow it,' she says. 'It's very simple. You see here? And here? All you do, and do it on a daily basis, please, is fill them in.' If this wasn't bad enough Orchid has it in for Christopher.

'I couldn't manage without him,' Mrs Brande insisted. 'He's really interested in catering,' she says, though Christopher isn't interested in anything at all. Bloody woman, how could Orchid know anything about children, about the temptations of a seventeen-year-old? If you pay tax at all you should be bloody grateful that I look after him, she would like to say. It wasn't easy having Christopher under her feet at work but without her to watch over him . . . Orchid hasn't mentioned William, no one has, but Mrs Brande feels like mentioning him when she sees those yellow forms. She would like to tell Orchid about the day he came all soaking wet to her canteen and how she did a fry-up for him, but how could she, when fry-ups were frowned upon? She got a very hard look from Miller when she served him avocado and it wasn't just the chaplain who received the full-coloured, A3 photocopy of celery. Mrs Brande got three.

'From now one I have no intention of talking to anyone,' Dee told Eddie. 'Far too dangerous. If anyone says a word to me about William I shall pretend I haven't heard them. My response will be short and to the point: "William? William who?"'

A track runs from the drying racks to the Nubrite washing-machine, from the Nubrite to the windowsill, from the windowsill to the canvas sacks of laundry. Dee would go down on her knees and sniff that track just for the scent of Eddie. And there is a gap now that William has gone, an aperture. A little dip. Dee could sing now that she has seen it, a little gap that she can snuggle into. 'Not that the freshly dead don't linger. I've seen him several times myself, slipping round a corner . . . and there's always a doubt, isn't there, when someone dies, a question mark, especially in here. And they didn't ring the bell this time, Eddie, did you notice that? Not like when Sheila went, doyng, doyng, doyng, doyng . . .'

The weather is marvellous, or that is how Dee sees it. After the November rains December is crisp and dry and bright. And it makes her feel buoyant; the east wind that makes the others shudder sharpens up her wits. Each afternoon the low sun turns the sky a livid yellow.

'I adore these cold crisp days, don't you, Eddie?' she says, joining him on his walk up to the windowsill. Soon she will take his arm as easily as she takes Maisie's arm. There is a gap, but it strikes her now that it is all too reminiscent of the dent in Miller's leg.

'I suppose one might glean pleasure from even the grimmest in our company,' she says, referring to the fact that Miller now shares Eddie's table in the canteen. 'Hubert was very fond of Miller, though, of course, he was not bisexual, well, too exhausted to be sexual at all, poor lamb. Nevertheless I did trust his judgement, still do. He's with us in spirit, you know, Eddie, I sense he's there, watching over us, just slightly the worse for wear. I feel buoyed by Hubert, Eddie dear, don't you?

'Personally I have to say that the allure of Miller totally escapes me. I've always considered him . . . or not considered him . . . But all is never completely lost, I suppose. There is always the possibility of being stung into memory by a late wasp. One only needs a prod . . .' Dee would like to unzip Eddie's trousers and have a peek at what is inside them. 'My affections are elastic, Eddie, my friendship with Maisie is not exclusive, do remember that.' A prod in the right place, she muses, a baptismal dunking or in Miller's case an electronic goad.

'I meant to ask you, Eddie, did William leave anything at all for us to remember him by?'

'Everything and nothing,' Eddie says.

For William's suicide has greased the slide and the longing to simply go, whizz down, be done with it, grows in PAIN like a contagion. Dee will witter on, but the rest are silent, for one and all can see the slide as clearly as if it had been erected in the Airing Court for public view. Bullit sniffs around the base of it, the structure glistening beguilingly in the early morning frosts, suggests a cocking of the leg. High it stands, turned livid yellow in the low sun of afternoon . . . 'Lethargy & Temptation' embroidered on the little cushion at the top.

Fatty Barrett spits at the cross sections of the brain and rubs them with his shirt-sleeve and Paula's stapler has gone missing. These days when she turns her photo cube it is William's face she sees. Christmas is coming and Dr Beaker is constructing a canoe in his office. When questioned he insists his son will see it if he does it in the shed. This morning Orchid snagged her red tights against the frame. 'I'm taking it out of petty cash,' she informs Paula, and Paula agrees she may as well stock up.

Shut away from tripe and trivia Swan, resolved to beating the blip into a pulp single-handed (his present area of research is solates), writes with his back turned firmly from the slippery slide. If his eyes stray at all it is to his credentials framed upon the wall. Though cold air whips the last remaining leaves from the trees, in the mansion of Swan's head – when he makes this kind of effort – it is always summer and the prospect is both lovely and invigorating. The smell of salt has blown in on the breeze, on the waves that roll towards him from across the great Pacific. In shorts and sandals Swan writes to the beat of the pounding of the waves upon his private shore, the bloom of fresh fruit on his desk, from the back of the stilted house somewhere the smell of freshly ground coffee. His warm skin is cooled by the graceful revolutions of a fan that flutters the pages, of air tickets tucked beneath an anglepoise . . .

'Major cock-up,' Beaker says, pointing to an article about William in one of the Sunday papers. 'Probably up the spout.'

'I'm sorry?'

'Orchid. Not exactly on the ball,' he says, jabbing his finger at the newsprint.

Particles of rice cake, like bumper flakes of dandruff, adhere to Beaker's beard and moustache and snail trails of glue glisten on his sweater. Like a bear he stands there, waiting.

'Hard-wired, if you ask me,' Beaker says.

Swan hasn't asked. He doesn't want to know. Put off his stroke by Beaker Swan makes an exit from his office, forced to set on an unplanned perambulation. So be it, but, oh dear me! Working in a sunlit glade plays havoc with the psyche. Leaving it and entering the interior of PAIN is like stepping out of a Monet into some dingy and dirty brown thing. The play of light is nowhere to be found in PAIN. Is it this, Swan muses, that bows the shoulders of the inmates so, that shackles their legs?

Only the entrance hall is to his taste and Swan loses himself for a while among the faces of his predecessors. Hung so high they appear to him, as they would have wished to appear, supremely unassailable. His portrait will take its place among them soon, though how long it will hang is now debatable. Still, he can use the image for the backs of book jackets, he can hang it in the hall at home if it isn't needed for the nation. In a couple of months Swan's papers will be collected into a book and he will be free to sign copies. He can see himself settled at a small table, flourishing his fountain pen. Armed with this vision he is able to move more briskly through the building, dealing manfully with the swing doors, his heels clicking impressively on the stone and brick, hands clasped behind his back, smiling and being smiled at. Miss Swift asks her class to stand when he enters – he likes that – and he smiles through the glass partition at the chaplain rehearsing with the Christmas choir. Obviously the blip is quite invisible, it is pure pleasure for his staff to see him, he must do this more often. No doubt Ivan Clampit perambulated, and Jocelyn Jocelyn, and Hilary Shadbolt and Robert Wilder; only Hubert stayed in the office, too unsteady on his legs. Walkabouts were an obligation that Swan had overlooked. The canteen was a possibility, surely, the captain dining now and again with selected passengers and staff. Now an inner glow almost eclipses the newspaper article and the threat of neuroscience, even the earlier unpleasantness with Julia. A fax had come in overnight offering the possibility of a conference in Mexico City. Cheered by the prospect he had tried to kiss his wife as she left before him for her office. He had clutched at her hand but she had shaken him off. 'Not now, Michael!'

If not now then when?

The Airing Court was empty. He was alone, or thought he was, thinking of Julia – Lord deliver us, surely she wasn't expecting him to say sorry! – when he was surprised to feel a restraining hand upon his arm. How he had missed the owner of that hand he would never know. A huge man in charge of a wheelbarrow. In fact it wasn't a hand that grasped him at all but two small planks of wood used for leaf gathering. And the wood was held by what looked like a tramp, of all things. It took a while to shake the tramp off and even when he freed himself he felt imprisoned by the look in the man's eyes.

After this he couldn't get out of the court quickly enough, the touch of Miller awakening him well and truly to the cold air and the dry swirl and rustle of the leaves. Swan sensed the man's eyes boring into his back as he made swiftly for the first available door.

Wet warmth engulfed him now; there was so much steam that it took a moment to make out the creatures in the room. A cat ran between his legs and on top of a vibrating machine a tin of tobacco shimmied closer and closer to the edge. Swan put his hand out to steady it and steady himself.

In the room a fine-looking man stood reading by the windowsill and a sturdy woman sat smoking, her feet along a bench. Once again there was, thank God, an appropriate reaction to his presence – at least from one of them. The man left the book and came towards him.

'Look what the cat's brought in,' the woman said.

'Still going strong,' Swan addressed the Nubrite Industrial Washer.

'Nineteen seventy-four,' said the man.

'Don't stop. Don't let me to disturb you. I expect we'll be seeing you both in the department shortly —'

'No one said —'

'Goodness me. Nothing to worry about. What I meant . . .'

'William stole one of my earrings,' Dee said. 'It would be reasonable, I think, to have it back?'

'A dreadful tragedy.'

'You can't wear one,' said Dee.

'May I offer you a cup of coffee?' the man asked.

'That's very kind, but I think . . .' The machine started up again. 'Noisy beast,' Swan said, withdrawing. 'Asthma,' he said. 'Cold air then into the hot air . . .' A bell rang shrilly as he made his way out of the door.

There were more people in the Airing Court now, but Swan could clearly pick out the man who had accosted him. There. Standing head and shoulders above the rest.

Prennely approached him.

'Morning, sir.'

Swan indicated the man.

'It's Miller, sir, or Mr Miller, as we are told to call them now.'

'Miller?' Swan didn't know they had a Miller. 'Miller? Are you sure?'

Quite appalling, whatever his name was, this dinosaur in the middle of the court, this grizzled ancient! An image from some hoary past that the department had somehow overlooked. This was mould, this was detritus! This was an eyesore that must be dealt with, swamped at once by a

145

bucket of scalding disinfectant. Swan clung to his inhaler, taking a second squirt as he travelled back up in the lift to his department. Like the hulk of an old boat . . . Miller?

'I'd like to see Mr Miller some time this week, Paula.'

'Miller?'

'Yes, Miller. That's what I said.'

'It was a turquoise scarab,' Dee said. 'Not that he hung around long enough for me to point that out. And I know exactly how it got to William, I can chart its progress. It may be small but it means a lot to me, anyone with a human nature would understand my need to get it back. Sheila took it.' Dee took the spoon out of Maisie's hand and relieved her of her cup of tea. 'Then it's up, down and how's your father. Are you listening to me? Sheila, Eddie, William, Maisie, that's the track we're on and now I've only one earring and I'm hardly a hippie. You can't wear one. The point is that if I was to have a . . . session . . . with someone, then I'd like to wear those earrings. Not just any-one, Maisie, someone . . . someone of our own class, dear, from the plateau, so to speak. It's not simply a knowledge of where I'm placed in the world but that I absolutely know that I have nothing whatsoever in common with these blow-ins and -outs we see so much of these days in here. It would have to be someone in the hierarchy, Maisie, some-one who knew things, who knew Hubert, someone who cared about things the way we do. There's only so much one can get from a letter,' she says wistfully. 'Or from stroking Bullit's fur. I need to be looked up to, not down on. It's hardly my fault that I've never set foot in a super-market or couldn't answer questions on the Vietnam war. Not having used a cash dispenser does not disqualify me from living. But really, what I have got to say to someone whose brain has been jangled by an acid trip or a religious sect in Gobi?

'Goa,' said Maisie.

'Was it? I couldn't be bothered to listen. Such girlish hair, like the Laughing Cavalier. No, it would have to be someone . . .' Dee looks across the canteen to where Eddie is sitting with Miller.

'Miller?' asks Maisie.

'No, Eddie, you idiot.'

'Will you get rid of the dog, then?' Maisie asked her.

'Don't be ridiculous,' said Dee.

Dobie would have taken Miller straight up to Dr Swan but Prennely was a kinder man. Prennely saw to it that the corners of Miller's mouth were wiped and took a pair of sharp nail scissors to the gorse that sprouted from his nostrils and his ears. So close was Prennely to Miller that he could hear his old heart beat, could see a faint green line around his neck, a legacy of Hubert's watercress treatment. Miller's hair could not be subdued and wetting it proved fruitless.

'Better with or without?' Prennely asked Dobie. It was decided that Miller should carry the fez. Miller yawned then and Prennely saw to his dismay that it was far too late for flossing or for fluoride. Should he say, 'Don't open your mouth'?

Preparations too were being carried out in the psychiatry department. Should the team be seated informally, apparently discussing something cerebral and Miller's visit greeted as a pleasant interlude? Should they wear their white coats for easier identification, should they look importantly preoccupied? What should they look like? Like Robert Wilder in the photograph: less a doctor, more a friend? What did they actually look like when they looked like themselves? Should Swan sit at his desk or stand in front of it? He practised it both ways. To get from the handshake and back behind the desk in one fluid movement . . . they might need an officer on hand. It would have to be Prennely – a pity they had got rid of that big boy Warren . . . Miller was not on any stupefying drugs, they had checked, and he could be – what was the word they used to use for it – obstreperous, bolshie? Volatile, that was it. Behind the desk, thought Swan. Being up here might be disconcerting to someone used to different climes . . . and only at the last minute did Swan remember to alert the team that no one was to mention the escape. Miller had probably forgotten it and rubbing salt into an old wound was not advisable with a . . . volatile . . . man. 'Don't mention the escape,' Swan memoed his department. 'Shred after you've read.'

The three psychiatrists talked among themselves, better to talk than to be read by one another. Swan straightened his cuffs, Orchid smoothed her tights, Beaker farted sadly. How extraordinary it would be to see Miller. Why had they put it off so long? They looked anxious, claiming to each other that the anxiety was excitement. What would Miller say? What would they say to him?

Never apologize.

Should they explain?

Never explain.

They would have tea. Tea would be a consolation for the fifty-eight-year wait. The chance to take tea with a relic was, as Orchid said, so real. Swan briefed Paula on the tea, flexing – it was painful – the atrophied muscle of his imagination. Miller would like strong brown tea with several sugars, the spoon must stand up in the cup. The tea would be drunk sitting down – but do you put a Miller on a sofa?

You do not. It was someone else's fault, of course, that the furnishings in the department seemed now so totally inappropriate. What one needed for a Miller, and Swan wanted one brought now, at once, was a hard-backed chair. And it was finally decided that, whatever the risk, Swan, as leader of the team, must be as courageous as he was gracious. Yes, Swan would come out from behind his desk, ask Miller to sit down in the hard-backed chair then go – not retreat, go – not quickly but calmly, no scurrying; he would melt back behind the desk.

The actual moment of arrival is always swift after so much waiting. Swan was just considering eats – bread and dripping might be just the thing – when Miller was ushered in to the department. Miller was there and they need not have worried, for the old man came straight out with a compliment.

'Dulcet,' he said.

He shook their hands sombrely. It looked as if he might kiss Orchid's hand: he raised it to his lips, then dropped it. They said hello and Beaker, who had sat inadvertently on the hard-backed chair, levered himself up and said, 'How's it going, mate?'

Miller looked around.

'The green's disconcerting you, isn't it?' said Swan. 'Looking for those old brown skirtings, the grey filing cabinet. New is good, Miller, and green is what the doctor ordered. Had to be radical. And green isn't as easy as it sounds, you know, so many hues.'

Hughs? Miller made a waggling gesture with his long, blue-veined hand. They stared at the hand, willing themselves to interpret the waggle. He did it again, several times, waggle, waggle.

'Fish!' cried Orchid.

'If you will do the honours, Beaker?' said Swan.

The fish were brought in, trundle, trundle. Miller looked into the tank, made the sign of the big one.

'Where is the big brute?' Beaker looked accusingly at Swan. Now it was Swan's turn if not to waggle his hands then to open his palms and shrug, to change the subject.

'Now. Please everybody. Do sit down.'

Somehow Swan was not where he should have been, behind the desk, but never mind that. He tapped an old buff file and flipped the first page open. Miller's name was written on the first page of the file in flowing copperplate. Miller looked at the name. His writing was big in those days – or was it someone else's writing? Swan picked up the file and carried it back behind the desk. He flicked through its pages quickly, past the failed surgery (particularly upsetting was the mastectomy, the consequence of a course of hormone treatment).

'We don't need to go into any of this,' Swan said. 'Water under the bridge, old man.'

Miller gazed out of the window. This was a view he hardly knew. A iron bench curved round a tree of heaven that still had a few of its leaves. A big fat jay was sitting in its branches.

'I often look out of the window myself,' said Swan. He was aware of an unusual emotion he couldn't quite put a name to: an emotion that affected the muscles in his neck and made him want to bow his head. It wasn't very nice. What should a younger man say of this file, this life? To part of it he might say, 'My man, you brought it on yourself', but really this was no thirty-five-minute tunnel, this was definitely no blip. He thought of the last play he had seen with Julia, his anxiety during the final act that the playwright might not manage to get his characters successfully off the stage. The unusual emotion made him feel uncomfortable. Moreover, for once he couldn't think of anything to say.

'Coffee or a glass of water?' Beaker offered.

No! Miller would think Swan was about to prescribe! Swan buzzed Paula. 'Tea!'

'You don't mind Dr Beaker and Orchid sitting in, I hope? You have met, I take it? Oh dear. Now let me see, you knew Dr Bottril, of course?'

Miller continued to gaze out of the window.

'Are you fond of autumn?'

Miller turned his gaze to Swan, unsure if he had heard autumn or Orchid. If he answered correctly would they let him go?

'Perhaps,' Swan said, 'I could show you around the department while we're waiting for your tea. All change, you know,' he went on, slipping bravely out from behind the desk. 'Change is the stuff of life.'

A loud crack from the hard-backed chair, Beaker had bloody broken it. Oh yes, that would be just the ticket, Miller grabbing a bit of chair and threatening them all with it and no one on hand to help. Swan rose to the occasion, guiding Miller slowly out into the foyer. The others followed.

The fax machine, the mineral-water machine, the photocopier; Miller was non-committal about these, but the pictures of the brain in section caught his eye.

'Where's the other one?' he asked.

Swan pulled a face at the others.

'It's a cross-section, Miller.'

Miller tapped his chest where his heart was. They didn't understand. Swan pointed out a pale-blue synapse and a couple of neurons on the coloured print. He waved at the others to get back into the office; he wanted a chance to talk to Miller on his own.

'Look,' he said to Miller. 'I hope there's been no misun-

derstanding. I wouldn't want you to think . . . just famili-
arizing ourselves with each member of our small
community. Putting names to faces, you know how it is.
Just wouldn't want you to think . . . or to have thought
before you came up here that we were going to . . .
Everything will go on just the same, you see.' He coughed
and touched his own chest. 'Asthma,' he said and cleared
his throat. 'By this stage I expect you've got your own . . .
façon de vivre, Miller? Wouldn't wish to upset the old routine.'

'Tea for Mr Miller?' Paula said.

'I think we'll take it in my office, thank you, Paula.'

Miller sipped his tea but did not say, 'Just how I like it.'

Never mind. Now all four looked out of the window.
Silence.

This meeting, Swan thought bitterly, had been badly
managed after all. The psychiatrists looked one to the
other. Miller drank his tea. What Swan should have done
was preordained an ending. There should have been a
phone call, a fire drill . . . Miller drank and when he had
drained the cup he put it very carefully upon Swan's desk
and once more, but gently this time, touched his heart.

'Iswungen,' he said and they did not understand.

A pre-arranged signal, Beaker's roll-up setting off the
smoke alarm . . . In desperation Swan buzzed Paula. Once
he had buzzed the rest came easily.

'This has been so useful,' he said to Miller, scribbling
'Why don't we do this more often?' on a piece of paper and
handing it to Beaker.

'Why don't we do this more often,' said Beaker.

'It's been lovely,' said Orchid.

'Terrifically valuable,' said Swan. 'Getting together and
talking, what is psychiatry if not interactive, Miller?'

Miller can't answer that.

152

'So. Back to the grind,' Swan remarks, passing him over to Prennely, tapping Miller on the shoulder, raising a great cloud of dust.

The ground is frozen hard now and the bare trees stand fixed and open-branched in supplication. December fairly zips along. Everything and everyone is on the move. Though Dee has told Verne on so many occasions, to mark her words, 'That bad neck is truly your best ally. They'll never move you in that condition,' they have. Ridout, too, has gone and in Miss Swift's sadly depleted soft-toy class Fatty Barrett takes over snake and duck. Now it seems that Dee too is targeted. Orchid has left several messages for her to get in contact and this evening Orchid turns up in the sitting-room of Roma for a chat.

A little holiday is what she is suggesting. Restorative, she says, meaning rehabilitating. A small bed and breakfast in the west of the country, in a village, on a main road, near a bus stop to the town. Dee won't hear of it; in fact, she literally blocks her ears. Holiday is code for the lime-pit. Dee reaches for the remote control and turns the television on.

'I can't stay for long,' Orchid says, though she looks drained, feels drained, has not the energy to rise from the small armchair. So she is drawn into the scene on television, documenting the attempted rescue of a small dog stuck down a well. Firemen fill the screen, interspersed with the dog's loving family who ritually come back and forth, peering into the well's dark circle. The dog's barks have not been heard for three-quarters of an hour. There is just a chance that it has gone to sleep. The season is summer and a small child has brought out all the dog's playthings, which she arranges on a blanket then sprinkles with Good Boy Dog Chocs, now melting in the sun. Seeing how the broadcast might go Dee has taken the precaution of shutting Bullit in the cupboard.

'Tosca, Tosca, Tosca!' call the family and the firemen. Orchid's eyes are pricked with tears.

Prennely insists that Miller stay indoors these cold days. He has not been himself – whatever that is – and Prennely is concerned that he might get a chest infection or worse. Exercise remains important and Prennely sits at one end of the long gallery in the Wet Weather Room, allowing Miller the full length to walk around. 'I can see the way things are going even if you can't,' Prennely's wife says to him daily. 'Don't think they'll thank you for your loyalty.' She is very cross with Prennely at the moment. She doesn't like the way that PAIN has treated Warren and she wants her husband to apply for a new job. There are all sorts of jobs open to man in his position with his experience. She won't let him alone. Her bullying is interspersed with a tenderness that he finds cloying and no matter how cold the last few days have been he has spent as much time as he can out in his shed.

Security guard, traffic warden. He could do anything with his record of trust and responsibility. 'You've got to be more of a self-starter,' she insists. She has taken it upon herself to find him something, urging him to fill in applications, putting this and that in front of him. Would he fancy being a green keeper on a golf course, part-time and very cosy; a cottage with a garden that leads down to a holly orchard goes with the job. She likes the sound of that. 'You could be your own boss, Frank,' she says but he doesn't want to be his own boss and the cottage looks poky and he is used to long windows, huge rooms . . .

While Prennely ponders the classified columns Miller

trudges round the gallery. He has stripped his shirt off, but Prennely doesn't notice this. On and on goes Miller, setting up a rhythm for his thoughts. The shirt is his marker. Each time he treads on it he starts to think again, then loses the thought before he gets round to the shirt again. If Jesus would only look down, if Jesus would only look down.

For half of the circuit he can think, for the second half he loses himself in a cross-hatched grid. If death were to come prematurely . . . if Jesus would only look down. Thousands went out to join Jesus in the desert, each one taking sand to build the pyramids of forgiveness, yet they wore the sort of clothes that impeded their progress, clothes that others clung to. Miller's chest is bare, there is nothing more he can remove though he now tugs at his trousers. He lays his face against the mesh of wire that reaches from the gallery railing to the ceiling. To throw himself at the man's feet, he thinks, to extinguish himself and prove himself through dehydration. Hoofed up into the atmosphere by the camel caravan. Jesus and the disciples came, created a lot of dust in the atmosphere, kicked up sand that simply added to their stature. You could, if you like, see them coming . . .

Enough! Swan is only human, he needs help. On Friday afternoon Michael Swan leaves the department early and drives east towards a weekend with Gilbert, towards the possibility of breaking the circle of the blip.

The friary is set at the end of civilization as Swan knows it, with the sea licking about its edges as if to underline the point. The journey is long and Swan has a headache. He drives with lights and wipers on. It rains in squally bursts and as he flashes past the signposts the thought that in less that forty-eight hours he will be flashing past them in the opposite direction brings some relief. It was not feasible to pop in on Gilbert and in the telephone conversation with him Swan had lamely agreed to two nights, though originally he had seen it as one.

'Stay as long as you like.' Gilbert was magnanimous. 'Open house. You know the score.' Swan did know that to leave early looked bad, looked as if you couldn't take what was on offer.

The dark was very dark on the small roads that wound down to the friary. His lights picked up a monk feeding fodder to a donkey. He found that irritating. As the modern chapel came into view he found that irritating too. His perfect memory recalled each stitch of the hideous contemporary altar cloth, the orange and midnight blue of the futuristic cornfield . . . he would spend some time with Gilbert tomorrow, he would leave tomorrow night. The air smelt wonderfully fresh and salty, clouds moved swiftly over the moon. The donkey feeder showed him round his quarters, his sandals flapping against the quarry tiles of the converted goose house. Swan's attempt at small talk was aborted by the monk, who pointed to a notice on the wall requesting visitors to observe the monks' silence between the hours of 8 p.m. and 8 a.m.

The country in December. Swan shivered by the tiny washbasin and went to bed in socks. Windy, silent, cold. Swan lay in a strange and hard single bed unable to make believe for a moment that he was anywhere else but here . . . in Gilbert's clutches . . . Had he been a fool to come?

He was woken early by a noise he couldn't fathom; it turned out to be the thuggish pull of sheep at the grass beyond his window. Seven fifteen in the morning and through the window Swan could make out the glow of lanterns in the darkness, lights burning in the main house and the sounds of people already up and at it, the brothers going about their morning's work.

Naturally at this time of year there were no other retreatants in the goose house. Washed, dressed – Swan's country wear consisted of pale-grey cashmere V-neck and a quilted coat – and putting a brave face on it, he made his way to breakfast in the main house, to find its halls already milling with old men; ragged men who reminded Swan of Miller, men who dribbled into their beards with biblical exactitude. How could he have forgotten that the friary was a staging post for tramps?

A tatter of old overcoats preceded him into the breakfast hall. Brown tea with milk already in it, porridge decanted into every bowl. The meal was mercifully silent. A quick flick of the eyes showed no Gilbert. Swan looked into his cup and into his porridge, conscious of being stared at, conscious of being overdressed. Seven forty-five and he felt his face contract into a picture of recoil, distaste, yet he ate up his porridge, drank his tea, spread his toast with margarine.

Swan had left messages for Gilbert, but he hadn't seen him yet. This was no bad thing. Checking his face in the mirror at the goose house Swan hoped against hope that his old friend wouldn't see straight though him. Was it visible, this blip? And Gilbert would be on sparkling form, of course, his territory, revitalized by having spent the best part of the morning on his knees.

'So good to have you here again.'

Monks that Swan didn't recognize greeted him at every turn.

'Morning. Nice to see you. Bit blowy!'

The democracy of the establishments apparently gave every brother the right to address him as a long-lost friend. Swan didn't like it much. He presumed that they did it to everyone but he wasn't everyone, he was a very old and special friend of Gilbert's, he was Swan! The best bet was to appear preoccupied. Swan carried the notes on 'Disintegrating Personhood' under his arm and tried to look as if he meant business. He parked himself outside and sat stoically reading until he could bear the cold no longer and had to go back in. A bell rang for chapel. Monks were streaming from every direction and he was in their path, as they came running from the kitchen and the fowl yard, hurriedly pulling their cowls over their heads.

'Excuse me.'

'Sorry.'

Swan needed somewhere to read quietly. He had missed the moment, there was nowhere inside that hadn't been already occupied by tramps. Tramps were steaming in the library by the gas heaters, every burbling, gurgling fire had its token tramp; there were tramps sleeping in the sitting-room and snoring in the hall and beyond the steamed-up windows tramps worked with wheelbarrows in the kitchen garden with eager, young brown brothers fresh from Matabeleland. The view was tramps. Looking out of the window Swan watched a brown arm pull the starter of a chain saw. A stocky lad threw logs on to a pile as two others worked a crosscut. Axe and steel in the cold, bright, blowy morning. So it bloody went on. Tramps bundling kindling, stuffing sawdust into sacks, stirring pigs' swill. Out of chapel the brothers swished about between their fellow brothers, running around on the lightest of sandalled feet, their skirts gathered up above the mud created by so many heavy boots, rosaries swinging from their stout brown belts, bouncing on their strong, young, purposeful thighs.

Swan's bedroom had no lock. It was more like a cell than a bedroom and it was freezing cold. He shivered miserably on the edge of the bed. There was no sound from outside now apart from the squeal of gulls and when he had washed his hands to warm them up a bit he had heard the suck glug as the water went out and down the pipe.

'Swan, isn't it? How good to see you! Brother Gilbert said to expect you this weekend.'

Introductions to monks who Swan was sure he had never met before, introductions they saw as reintroductions. A lot of patting on the back and hand shaking.

'You remember Brother Ernest?'

He did not.

'Keith is working in the inner city now.'

Who the hell was Keith?

'Brother John has been seconded on to the Rural District Council. I know he'd love to pick your brains about the rural poor.'

'Not my patch, I'm afraid,' Swan said.

The monk put both arms round him in a hug. 'That's the point of this place, Mike, space to let the interface converge.'

Running away from them at walking pace was how Swan spent Saturday morning, back and forth to the igloo with its glugging plug.

'Where have you been hiding?' Gilbert let himself into the room.

'Here!' He threw a pair of wellingtons in Swan's direction. 'Fancy a walk?'

The old friends hugged each other. Gilbert's louche, urbane face had aged considerably, which cheered Swan up a little bit.

'Always frantic just before Christmas,' Gilbert said, obviously enjoying it. 'Come on, get the boots on. Have to get going at this time of year or you miss the light.'

The friends were the same age though Gilbert was fitter. He took off now along a sodden ash path through rows of cabbages and sprouts.

'Won't be a tick,' he said, darting across the rows to have a word with one of the brothers. Swan sat down and waited for him on a damp and mossy bench.

'Sorry about that.'

'Don't worry,' Swan said. 'I'm fine.'

Why had he said that? Was it paranoia or did he get the distinct impression that he was being looked after? Swan sprang from the bench as heartily as possible. Perhaps it wasn't the blip that Gilbert saw but simply that his friend was cold? Gilbert was without even a coat over his habit ... Trying to keep up academically with Gilbert had been difficult enough; following him across a field was tough. On they walked, absolutely freezing, rain now coming with the wind.

'We're all so interested in the work you're doing,' Gilbert said.

That was the difference between them, thought Swan. Gilbert who had always had ... who hid behind, perhaps ... the confidence of 'we', the confidence that Swan ought to have got from Julia?

'Of course, we can see here – mind, that stile is slippery – see the results of Care in the Community only too clearly. More disturbed people than ever on the roads.'

Swan was out of puff already. Gilbert raised his voice against the wind.

'Our local hostel has become a victim of the cuts and we simply haven't got the space for any more. You can see for yourself, Michael, chock-a-block. And the asylums are half empty, so we hear. Something wrong somewhere. Far too many youngsters on the road, that's the main change, dislocated youngsters . . .'

Swan, turning his ankle in a rabbit hole, felt pretty bloody dislocated himself. On they went along narrow furrows, the wind lifting the skirts of Gilbert's habit, crossing the deep fields towards the sea.

'Remember the walks we used to have? Always good to get out and have a blow in the fresh air. I still do it, you know, come out here and shout, to take the pressure off. Of course in the old days the problems usually revolved around women.'

'Still do,' Swan said.

Gilbert chuckled then, throwing his arms out wide, his habit blowing hard against his legs. 'Hear me, O God!' he cried.

Swan was embarrassed.

'Shout. Michael. Let it out, man!' The skirts of Gilbert's habit were clogged with mud and there he stood, waving his arms and actually jumping up and down. Not cold but joy or . . . the love of life without women to complicate it all? 'Come on, Michael, shout.'

Swan's teeth were chattering and he had sore lips. It was even colder right on the coast but at least conversation in this wind was virtually impossible. After what seemed an age walking the edge of the grey-brown sea they turned back. In this flat country Swan could see how far they had to go.

'Wind's at our backs now.'

It was still wind.

Gilbert took his arm.

Pin down?

'I was hoping to see Julia.'

'Difficult.'

'What sort of difficult?'

'Not difficult difficult, nothing like that.' Swan had

always pretended to Gilbert that he still loved Julia. Perhaps he did. 'It's just that she . . . I told her I was bringing some work down with me and she's very taken up with piano at the moment, steaming through the grades.'

'Hasn't changed, then?'

'Not a bit.' I'm the one who's had it. Swan longed to confide but couldn't find the words to do so. Anyway, it wasn't true, it was nothing, just a blip.

'Sorry to hear about your ma.'

'How's yours?' Swan asked.

'Full on,' said Gilbert with a wry look. 'Still batting for the other side, of course.'

Gilbert had been the butt of a great deal of teasing at their college. Gilbert the solid Marxist, with his mother publicly veering to the right of Ghengis Khan.

'Amazing energy, my mother,' Gilbert said.

Probably where you get it from, thought Swan.

'And your father?'

'Very happy,' Swan said. 'Really settled in.'

'And what have you been up to in that dreadful place? Time on your hands now, I suppose?'

'Papers to write.'

'I bet you long to get you hands dirty, don't you? Delve in.'

'Absolutely,' Swan said. 'Though naturally as one progresses in the profession so it gets more difficult.'

'I make a point of it,' Gilbert said. 'Won't take no for an answer. I just get up from my desk and get into the thick of it. It's the only way. You have to work alongside people if you're going to lead them, don't you think? Had a fight the other day, little bugger got me over the eye, here. Scrawny little chap too. Just trying to get a bottle off him and he clocked me. The one rule here is nobody drinks, that's all we ask. No alcohol. It's the only rule we've got and they have to stick with it, otherwise they're out on their ear.'

Now at last they were back on the ash path. It was too dark to see the cabbages now, only the white of cauliflower peeping through the murk.

'The demon drink,' said Swan, longing for it.

'The demon drink,' Gilbert repeated.

Swan remembered Gilbert throwing up into a basin very like the one he heard glugging in his freezing cell.

Gilbert took Swan's hands in his when they parted. It was dark and Swan wondered whether lack of confidence was like fear, something others could smell.

'One thing I should say is that you may experience some hostility here, Mike. I say may, because you never know and I wouldn't like you to be embarrassed. One or two of our unhappy wanderers have had experience of institutions. I imagine it's not something you forget. And the need to blame is universal, isn't it? Don't take it personally, but I'm sure you see the reasoning behind it. It's not enough to turf them out half-baked, is it, out with a prescription and a couple of pound coins. We can just about cope,' he went on, 'but only just.'

Swan nodded his head in the darkness, made all the right noises. He couldn't cope, but pride would not allow him to tell Gilbert that. He stood there in the darkness letting Gilbert have his say and wished that Gilbert did know, had smelt it, wished that Gilbert would help him.

I need help, I've had enough, help me . . . there was no way to phrase it, it was impossible to say.

'Musical evening tonight in your honour,' Gilbert said, clapping his hands enthusiastically, 'Shake the timbrels, pluck the harp.'

The acoustics of the Wet Weather Room make it difficult to distinguish individual sounds. Somewhere in the noise of the footsteps on the parquet, of the television and the ping-pong and the sponge darts, of the thud of demolition from Finisterre and the workmen's voices that sing and swear and whistle, in the hiss of the orange lights that burn all day, will be the sound from the surrounding forest of the felling of trees for Christmas. Out there in the woods the gateway is churned to muddy soup. 'Back up a bit. Forward. Back. Forward again now. Easy does it.' Cardboard, hardboard, a sheet of plastic spread beneath the wheels of the contractor's lorry, birds flying up into the cold sky, grey against the grey and the whoosh-thud of big trees falling.

Miller sits with Maisie. Neither of them talk. She sews in the poor light from the window, he grinds his teeth and stares into his hands. Flights of ideas are tabulated into columns that won't add up: sulphur, Lysol, alum, stag-well water, eye blinding, opium, arsenic, beeswax to polish, button hook to lever open . . . In a state of irritation he runs through the list again and again. Each word was a single, tired bird from somewhere in the Baltic on its way towards the sand of Africa, trying to find a quick way. These days he must not eat, however hungry. The chomping of his teeth magnifies the cacophony that is in his head.

'Come on,' says Mrs Brande in the canteen, but 'Come on' does not mean he is going anywhere. Miller sits by his pudding, the smell of pudding inappropriate. 'Come on. Come on.'

The canteen empties around Miller and Mrs Brande has that batch of yellow forms to fill. So he looks at the pudding, stirs it, closes his eyes and slips the spoon under the drawer in a different place. The drawer slides open.

Suffering always happens when someone is spooning pudding into your mouth . . . Mrs Brande takes the spoon from the pudding and begins to feed him, quite unaware that between mouthfuls the fruits of memory are dropping, dropping into his lap. Dropping like the peaches that drop on the grave of Conradi, the asylum's architect. With Mrs Brande about Miller cannot catch the fruits and they bounce about him, off the table, on to his kneecap, rolling round his feet.

'The Echelar Pass,' says Miller. 'After the Straits of Gibraltar. Beware the nets in the narrow break. If they don't get you going they will get you going back.' Birds appear to Miller, flying against a cold white sky and Hubert says it is unquestionably sporting. Silence is what Miller craves, not spooning. The hand that wags the finger warningly takes a hold of Mrs Brande.

Dr Swan hasn't said one word about decorations, but Paula has gone ahead anyway. Chinese lanterns hang on the back of the doors of the department, orange and blue foil streamers festoon the pictures of the brain. She stands on her swivel chair organizing, if not enthusing, Dr Beaker.

'Keep twisting.'

Paula bangs drawing pins into the green glade of the wall with the back of her stapler. 'Could you?' she asks of Swan as the phone rings.

It is a woman's voice. Beaker comes towards Swan, twisting, twisting. Swan moves out of his way.

'He was absolutely fine at supper.'

'What are you saying, Mrs Eversley?'

Mrs Eversley of Eventide is saying that Swan's father went out after supper yesterday evening and that he has not come back. Swan looks at his watch. Ten past eleven.

'I wouldn't phone only it looks as if he's taken his things, his asthma stuff . . .'

The chair that Swan wants to sink down on is being

stood upon by Paula. Swan leans against the wall, the picture of Paula's nephew smiling at him from the photo cube.

'Has something happened, doctor?' Paula asks him. 'Can I help at all?'

Swan replaces the telephone receiver and goes to get his coat.

'Are you going out?' she asks him. 'Will you be away long? Shall I say you'll be back later? This afternoon? Tomorrow morning?'

The phone rings again and Paula answers it, putting her hand over the mouthpiece.

'Are you taking any calls?'

Swan needs his wife for this one. He phones her from the car. Her secretary says she is out at the moment; would he like her to ask Mrs S. to call him back? On the mobile or at the office? Or perhaps at home? Wrong! Wrong! Julia should be at home sorting his socks out. Swan is an attractive man, why should he – damn it! – have to face this all alone?

By late afternoon Swan has done the rounds. He has driven to Eventide and back again, driven round the country roads and along the motorway, he has informed the police and told his sister Margaret; a great deal of activity but no progress at all. Now he sits in his study at home with his father's address book. He has driven halfway round the country to get it and not had any lunch. The book lies on the desk before him, closed.

It is strange to be home in the afternoon, with the smell of Julia's perfume that lingers in their bathroom, in their bedroom, on the stairs. His father has continued to use the family address book with its fifties idiocy of having to move a cursor down to a specific letter of the alphabet and depress a button in order to open the damn thing. Swan clicks A.

His mother's writing is efficient, neat, more like his. And his father's writing – how he must have irritated his wife even in this. Addresses are crossed out and overwritten, circled, arrowed, asterisked; noughts of telephone numbers are overwritten into eights and sixes. ABCD: the names of the mothers and fathers of the children he had played with and, it struck him now, frequently didn't like. Brankscome, Clive. Swan remembered the Brankscome ménage. Boys who thought it super fun to jump on your neck and bring you down in stinging nettles outside the poky cottage that fronted what was then a village green; the privy in the back garden where the pages of Wisden were used as lavatory paper; the joke that went with the Wisden and the privy: 'Always use Glamorgan first.'

ABCD: it all came back to Swan whether he wanted it or not. The clothes he wore were in these pages: the brown and green corduroy shorts that had a zip pocket on the right-hand side; the windcheater, also green, with the lining that flaked when you put your nail under it, with the lining that then caught in the zip. Swan was feeling cold, his feet were freezing, he wasn't meant to be home in the afternoon. The central heating did not kick in till after six.

'P', the woman with one eye lower than the other, whose husband had been in a Japanese prisoner of war camp. They had shared a house one holiday, before spillage from a tanker wrecked the beach. He rang the number, which came back as unobtainable. Dead? Gone? Or, like his father, wandered off?

Practising owl hoots through cupped hands on the drive to school; singing all the way along the wall that caged a big estate; sticking chewing gum in Margaret's hair; cutting through Swiss roll with toothbrushes on the evening that Mrs Tulloch babysat, gas at the dentist's; Chinese burns. Your mother sorted out your sock drawer, drove you home from the dentist if you had been given gas (she wouldn't let you take the bus). After gas you went to bed. Your father came up when he got back from the office, said you were his little chap. Fathers, Branscombes, Bullivants, Berkley-Smiths hidden behind newspapers, not to be disturbed. There nevertheless: fathers who mended bicycles and punctures, inflating inner tubes and holding them close to their whiskery faces, listening for the hiss, dunking the tubes in buckets of water from the outside tap, waiting for the bubbles; fathers who slung ropes up into the branches of trees; fathers who tried to kill themselves?

In this manner Swan reached 'R'. He couldn't bring himself to ring any of these people. These fathers, if they were still alive, did not go missing; these fathers from childhood were as staunch as Hemingways. They drank gin from tooth mugs in hotel bedrooms, they made you look them in the eye, they helped make dens, they put up tents, they bent skewers with their grown-up hands. They were there at airports and stations in duffle coats with money in their pockets; they were predictable, embarrassing and old-fashioned; they played Ray Coniff on the gramophone; they listened to the news; they said 'We'll see', to stall you, they packed the boots of cars with luggage – often in a bloody mood. They told you when they went away to be sure to look after your mother and your sister, that you were in charge of the house; they did not go anywhere without telling you, they came back when they said they would and even though it was frequently later than the time they had promised, they would always come and see you whatever time it was, look into your bedroom at night; they tucked you in then and when they had gone you rearranged the bed to suit yourself. 'Effort is more important than results,' they said; they were proud of you or disappointed in you . . .

'I want to come home.'

Swan steeled himself to ring a number. Incredibly a voice he recognized sounded at the other end.

'Michael! How lovely. What a surprise.' Lovely, though she had always preferred Margaret, every one had preferred Margaret.

'I wondered if he'd been in touch at all'

'No. Not for a long time. Nothing wrong, I hope?'

Julia would be back soon. She would open the lid of the piano, there would be the smell of her perfume . . . Hemingway had committed suicide.

Julia would want to know what on earth was going on. She would probably be cross. 'What on earth are you doing sitting here in the darkness?' or something like that. Julia would be home soon and Margaret would ring in and ask for a progress report. He had to include the possibility of the suicide of this man who had been at the station to meet him, stamping his feet against the cold, who had always waited even when Michael had missed the train. Mrs Eversley had said that she couldn't find, and so presumed that he had taken, his asthma inhalers and his Ventolin. That was not the action of a suicidal man.

'He was in your care.'

'I can't be held responsible —'

Only he was responsible.

'I want to come home.'

'Once your leg has mended . . .'

When his leg had mended he had gone off.

The phone rang. Swan let the ansafone take it. He heard Margaret's anxious voice, then a key in the door: Julia . . .

'Well done!' she said, putting her head round the door of the study. 'Cold in here. Why didn't you put the heating on?'

She went out again. From the kitchen he heard the click of the kettle, then her footsteps around the house. He wanted to run after her, hide his head in her skirt. He heard her open the fridge and close it again, then he heard her go upstairs and run water into the bath tub as he pulled himself stiffly from the chair to get a drink.

'You'd better get a move on, Michael.'

He didn't know how much time had passed when he heard her call again.

'Bath if you want it.'

Bath?

He had to tell her, she was calling down to him from the landing.

'I put these things out for you, Michael. Better get a move on if you're going to change.'

Bit late for that, he thought.

'Tell me what you think of this.' Julia stood at the top of the stairs looking extraordinary. He couldn't take it in.

'Remember this? Hot date with dead sheep?' Julia was wearing a knee-length Afghan coat. 'The Hulses' Christmas Party! I reminded you this morning. You said you'd come back early. Sixties' do. You'll never guess what I've dug out!' She waved a pair of yellow velvet trousers at him. 'And this, of course, lest we forget!' She held up a brown and cream Peruvian poncho. A set of elongated black-brown llamas raced unevenly around its long fringed hem.

'I . . .'

'Oh, come on!' Her voice had an edge to it now, he knew that she would be cross. She gathered up the clothes and shoved them at him. 'It's a spit roast. Outside. If you really can't stand the poncho . . .' Her voice trailed off into the spare bedroom, 'I suppose you could . . .' – she produced a ski jacket – 'at a pinch wear . . .'

170

'Julia —'

'Look, Michael. If you're going to muck me about I'm going on my own.

'You never enter into anything, do you? And now we're late on top of everything. I'm sick and tired of it, Michael. Your fucking mind is always somewhere else. I hate being late! I knew this would happen! And it's me, I suppose, who has to phone and say we're on our way.' Infuriated, Julia poked about in the darkness of the car. 'Where's the bloody phone?'

'In the back.'

She lent across him as he reversed out of the garage. Julia in the sixties, not wearing a bra.

'Takes you back, doesn't it?' said someone in a head-band and a beaded choker. Swan thought of an orange with a sugar lump stuck into it to stop the children moaning as they climbed back up a cliff. He thought of ice creams and wafers with his mother after a visit to the stocking menders, the small shop window that always fascinated him with its row of pinky-brown dismembered legs. He thought of baths with Margaret, of making Margaret eat the soap.

'I want to come home.'

'Michael!' Julia said. 'For Christ's sake, lighten up.' She grabbed a drink from a gingham tablecloth and shoved it into his hand.

The spit roast was taking longer than the book had said it would. The Hulses were distraught. The meat was burnt on the outside and raw inside, just how Michael felt. It was freezing hard, even with the barbecue; was his father out in this bitter cold?

'Isn't this fun!'

171

Inside now Swan danced drunkenly with a tall woman in a white and gold kaftan. However tall she was she must have shrunk – or Swan was totally plastered – as he kept treading, close to tripping, on her hem. Leaning against her for support he nuzzled his head against her chest and felt like staying there. She wasn't wearing a bra.

Dr Beaker has named his canoe after Preissnitz. Quiet in the glade on these days so close to Christmas. Paula has the afternoon off for shopping, while in Beaker's office Mrs Brande from the canteen now takes a stack of failures from her apron pockets and lays them on his desk.

Ah, so this is what it's all about! Dr Beaker, paint on his turn-ups, all fat and comforting, excavates and tunnels. Beneath the notes he finds Miller and beneath Miller is William, under William is Sheila Henderson and under Sheila lies a sediment of guilt.

'I blame myself, Dr Beaker.'

Never! In the grand history of PAIN, since the days of Josephine Foxley, since the hunt led out by Francis Weaver, portly in his scarlet coat, never has this phrase been uttered. It is sad that Swan is not around to witness the eclipse.

'I blame myself, Dr Beaker.'

As if once was not enough! Now the very ground beneath the building shudders. Daylight bulbs flicker a warning. 'Delete! Delete!' bleep the computers as the walls converge. The technicolour brain cross sections freeze to black and white and haemorrhage disgusting matter; tears gush from the mineral-water machine until, as if pulled by a centrifugal force, Beaker leaps athletically from his desk, nipping the word smartly between fat thumb and fat forefinger, dropping it scalding on the floor and, before it can breed, grinds it into the carpet, all his weight behind it with a heavy-healed, unpolished shoe.

Brande and Beaker are habitually red in the face, but what was once florid now turns magenta. Has Doreen placed herself in the world of untouchables? Will anyone speak to her ever again, ask her for a coffee or a currant bun? Was Nietzsche right or can miracles still happen? For softly, very softly, from somewhere close at hand, Mrs Brande hears a voice buzzing in her beehive, a voice that appears to sympathize, to understand.

From Dr Beaker comes the sort of noise that suggests an insight into days more sedate and certain, days when job descriptions were simply casual word of mouth. The dark age of which Mrs Brande is a graduate: of deep-fat frying; of holding a ladle steady and not flicking fag ash into the soup; of greasy-spoon cuisine that pivoted on white sliced toast; of multiplying by twelve on scraps of butter paper; of bulk orders of pork pies and pasties with no such thing as sell-by dates; of Aunt Daisy's hints from Tasmania – those crackly broadcasts on the crystal set – on how to preserve beetroot and remove scent marks from dressing tables; of when and where to dab household ammonia on the Masonic apron . . .

'It's not as if you just grilled a cutlet these days,' Doreen ventures.

And a hairy hand comes out towards the fair Doreen and declares that indeed it certainly is not. The world has moved on to diet sheets and calorie counts and roughage and irritable bowel syndrome, aloe vera drinks and sea-weed supplements.

'It's not enough,' she says, 'to flip a piece of breaded plaice.'

Cleanliness, cold cabinets and different types of yoghurt, it has all been mounting up. Dr Beaker shifts a gear though Mrs Brande – a blotchy white and scarlet, her eyes moist – is too distressed to see him do it. Rising from the desk he slides the blind down on the door, his paw dimming the controlled lighting.

'Relax.' The pressure on her shoulder blades is firm but gentle. 'Just lie back. Now, Doreen,' he says. 'You really are a wonder. Do you know I haven't had a battered sausage . . .'

And remarkably, for Dr Beaker is a remarkable physician, Beaker plucks Doreen from the abyss and back to the steady and familiar ground of recipes laid out like municipal park gardens. Confidence steadies the hand that will once again work the eyes out of green potatoes, sift white sugar across a sponge regardless of a line of grime beneath the fingernails. To gut a fish, to bone a chicken, to truss a turkey, to roll a filet of beef . . .

'And I'm worried about the inmates' Christmas dinner.'

'Oh, just defrost some thighs,' he says consolingly. 'It all comes in bags these days. My dear women, it's pointless, why resist? Oven chips can just be warmed and there are always nuggets. Tomato sauce, Doreen.'

Mayonnaise in Van Gogh yellow that comes in squeezy bottles. 'Prepared sauces,' Beaker says, warming to his subject. 'White pepper dust and ready-made curry powder need not compromise your pride.'

'I like to do it all myself,' she says, struggling against him, but he is far too strong for her.

'Doreen, Doreen, you porky little scratching, time to let go!'

No clocks in Beaker's room, no time. The lighting is low and in the murk she can see how Beaker has transformed his office into an extension of his garden shed. Through the gloom she picks out the Preissnitz canoe and the pliers on the filing cabinet, the tacks sprinkled, twinkling on the carpet, a paintbrush hardening on the mouse mat and – surely that wasn't there when she came in? – half a pasty warming on the radiator.

So he woos her, woos her.

'And I have reason to believe that Christopher has pocketed some teaspoons.'

'Forget Christopher, Doreen.'

Beaker listens, Doreen talks, just the two of them together. Out comes the roly-poly pudding that first Sheila, and now Miller, won't eat up. Out comes the fry-up made for William Carter, the admiration for Frank Prennely, the despair about the caravan. The fear of being followed home by Fatty Barrett, the fear of feathered men of twenty winters lurking at the bus stop hiding in the trees, the fear of Miller's grasp upon her reddened hand.

'And I always thought he was such a lovely man.'

It was Christopher, her son, who had summoned help that morning. Beaker says that Christopher will get a proper part-time contract if the institution should continue to operate into the New Year.

'And the teaspoons, doctor?'

'Look at this,' says Beaker, pointing a fat finger towards the feature that is obscured by moustache and beard. 'My lips are sealed, Doreen.'

It has all come out on Beaker's carpet, it has spread across the floor; personal responsibility and blame – that five-letter word that has been haunting her – all absorbed by an edifice built to absorb, deny, defend itself. Relief becomes wings on which to soar down to that bus stop, but until then Doreen at last has time to dream. Unlimited time for a one to one with Dr Beaker, Doreen hovering, weightless. Doreen is abstracted, is wandering, and what a delightful sort of wandering it is: a woman gathering flowers for a tussie-mussie, gathering, not picking or plucking but gathering, as he, listening, gathers her in.

And in this dreamy state brought on by canoe glue and radiator warmth and dim, dim lighting Doreen feels or thinks she feels the sun's rays warm upon her back. It is May again, she is young again and her limbs feel free and easy as Beaker draws her out and on and on, organically, like rosemary in warm water loosening a deeply embedded thorn. Time with Beaker is deliciously hypnotic, time means nothing and Doreen, uninitiated into the ways of doctors of the mind, has no inkling that the day has already passed its fair meridian, that the flowers in her hands are closing, that it will soon be dark and that she is far from home.

And Miller has been locked away, alone.

'You've been asking for this, Miller,' Dobie says and it is true, he has been asking, meekly and violently asking. Still irritable, still fasting, Miller savours the silence. He takes his clothes off and has to be restrained when he is dressed again. He must remove everything that gets in his way for he finds it easier to listen naked as the day that he was born. Miller is – or was at some time – a good servant. He has witnesses to prove it, documents attesting to his character, references that no one wants to hear.

These days and nights a dialogue absorbs him, but the words are indistinct and he must apply himself to them with total concentration; words from a seething pot, words from a quiet fermentation, gentle words that bloom into life in the nudge between green cooking apples putrefying on a pantry shelf. News comes at last to Miller from the great unpopulated wastes of China. Naked and alone he strains to hear it, for even in here in isolation there is always interference, jamming; so he stands naked in the centre of the room that he is locked into, every sense alerted to translate while he still has the energy, to decipher and at last to understand.

'He is a great servant of God,' the voice says, 'and he has taken up his abode in the bathroom. I do not know why he has chosen me, for I am more wicked than others and wholly covered with sins as a mangy dog with fleas. So I cannot tell why it entered his mind to live with me. He has fixed upon me and now lives with me. We cannot account for him with our thoughts and so we can understand only by signs. He is, in truth, a great servant.'

Miller talks and as he talks he gestures, tells of the Bath Mat in History where his mother laid him down. Locked away he addresses the silence about him with great courtesy. He enunciates with exquisite precision, speaking with slow deliberation, sure at long last of the chronology that made him Miller, aware at all times of the need for tact.

'My mother had begun to change my linen. I cried indeed but this was no more nor less than token protest, for it was a familiar disturbance and pleasant afterwards and only infuriating if it were cold or if she had woken me to do it, or if she did it in a rush, yes, or a bit roughly, yes, and if she failed to play with me at all during the proceedings. So she began to change my linen and then something . . . I can't say.

'She went from the room. I do avow that then I cried in earnest but I remember stopping before the crying tired me out. My eye was caught by how the light from the sinking sun illuminated the black casing of the bath, waving lines of water light. Above my head too there was some interest, late summer, August or September, and an insect with long fine legs struggled from a web that dangled. And I think too that there must have been some other sweet diversion in that bathroom, that perhaps in her hurry my mother had left something else of interest within reach. I think this must have been the case because I now remember that, though I was a crier like all babies, at this point I did not cry so very much. Something else that I cannot now specifically remember, something that held my attention but when my attention was sated I began to notice how very cold the room was and simultaneously I noticed the silence all around.

'No mother laughing in the kitchen, not her voice suggesting something, her voice half-way down the stairs. No hiss from the gas jet, strike of match, rush of water, clang of kettle against the stone edge of the sink. I listened then as I listen now and perhaps this is where my life of listening started. Listened for the hiss the kettle makes, the gathering sound before the kettle whistled and the little narrow window misted with steam. No curse at the dog or at the big ones in the alley, silence to which, in my limited way, I tried to find an explanation. The baker's boy or the coal man in his leather waistcoat, someone or something half-way down the street?

'Nothing then but silence, cold and frustration. When you can't move on your own and the bottle you're not meant to have is out of reach, not out of sight, cooling on an Everest of chair or chest of drawers . . . that, I see, was the point of interest in the bathroom, but I lost interest in it after what I'll call "a while". The sun had set and the crying hard had tired me and no one came and my crying took on a new note, which was fear. A note that stops the crying because it frightens the crier, as if it were the cry; that in changing its note alerts the heart and mind to the true significance of the situation. I hear it now, that cry, with its premonition of disaster: that no one will come. She is not coming, they are not coming, they have not even started off to come.

'Hunger begins as a preoccupation; though it becomes

obsession, there is plenty of space between the two. And in that space the door swings open and the dog comes in and the dog begins to lick me and I promise mutely to the dog that I will never make a fuss again. Never will I pull hair, or bite or kick and the tears when mother comes will be tears of relief, not anger. I defecate and urinate and begin to suffer pain from hunger, the pain I later suffered on the pyramid. Another pain assaults me now, a longing pain that comes off my skin, that holds the memory of touch of other skin and lips upon it. The pain of hunger and the pain of loss – that no one will come, will ever come – predominates. I see I am not worthy of her loving, she does not want my little arms. If anyone loved me it would be their mistake and they would soon discover it and stop.

'Small eyes open in the darkness, then another dawn, day, afternoon and the light on the bath and what was discomfort yesterday is pain today, acute and stabbing, so that I draw my dirty legs up in convulsion. Then this too passes as the dirt cakes and in its place is one red-rimmed anger and beside it one white peace ellipse. Anger becomes peace like an object inside you that is showing both its faces. A peace that is a dream of dying and an anger that is serrated by the rage of jealousy. Where are the arms of my mother, who should be holding me? A peace is a stupor, a rage interferes, a rage that is too much effort to sustain. Now a long pain eclipses both emotions, dulls plaintively to 'hold me', a label swings in the wind before the clouds burst, 'Heartbroken' reads the label and anyone would want to stop that pain.'

It is disconcerting, she can't bear it, waiting in the Airing Court without Maisie.

'Horrid, horrid, horrid.' Dee stamps and stamps her

feet. The gable clock strikes nine and then the quarter. Will no one ever come, will no one ever come, have they not even started off to come to pick her up?

Maisie is still in bed. Apparently it doesn't matter, nothing matters any more. 'Let her lie,' the new young lady said.

At last Dobie puts in an appearance and as he walks Dee to the laundry she has half a mind to take his arm. She won't, though; why give him the satisfaction? Dobie is not her type – a tall, a horrid little man. Her man, Eddie, is standing by the window, looking through it, watching as she approaches, for today there is no steam.

The door of the Nubrite Industrial gapes open. Eddie has something that he conceals from her. Well, so be it. Dee proceeds to her machine. With glasses on she threads it up; how prescient she has been all these months, the pile of pockets to be mended. A clever woman will always have her work beside hert.

She pauses before sewing, watching Eddie. The object in his hand is a small oilcan. He is oiling the castors of the drying racks, slowly and methodically, one by one. He is going soon, perhaps this morning, perhaps tomorrow, to a hostel in the city run by Spanish priests. His hands shake as he oils the little wheels, apprehension at what may be. His tired brain memorizes the introduction:

'Hola.'

'Buenos dìas.'

'Una habitaciòn, por favor.'

'Dos personas?'

'Una persona.'

'I'm considering giving up smoking,' Dee says in the act of lighting up. 'It detracts from the persona, don't you think? Important to choose one's moment . . . but I am seriously considering it, I thought you ought to know.

Hubert always said that in my case smoking was a mannerism and not an addiction . . . actually I was thinking, Eddie, that we might give up together. Would you be up for that?'

Eddie's face is turned away from her, the oilcan on the floor beside him. He pulls out the drying racks and they slide smoothly on their castors and her heart goes out to him, right out to him, right out across the laundry floor. How glad she is of the pile of pockets, of Eddie wandering round the room now, closing the cupboard door that always did swing open, back to the drying racks to collect the oilcan. She notices how much his hands are shaking as he places the oilcan up on the high shelf.

'The point is,' Dee says, 'that it may well be *de rigueur* when I get a new position . . . I imagine they'll probably come up with a new position? Obviously I can't say yet. Something appropriate to my experience; Orchid going clears the way. This' – Dee indicates the empty washing-machine, the Airing Court – 'is an interim period for me. I'm fortunate to be in a position to negotiate, you see. Naturally even I didn't really envisage . . .' – again she makes the gesture of taking in everything that is now nothing – 'Well, how could one? Don't cry, sweetie. Please, Eddie, don't cry. There are going to be a lot of new people. Not our sort, obviously, but new people and we'll rub along, won't we? You and me. With or without the cigarettes! And the thing is we'll be right at the top of the tree, well, obviously . . .'

She can't go to him, but she stands up anyway. A group of suited men she has never seen before are talking by the walnut in the Airing Court. One holds a clipboard, another mouths into a small tape machine.

'Maisie says it's *en suite* bathrooms and I wouldn't be surprised. I mean, they wouldn't have put the lights up last year – how much do you think that cost, Eddie? – or the CCTV. Everyone will have a little room, I think it's the Geneva Convention, three-sided with a curtain that runs across. I told Orchid I was perfectly happy with the skirting boards, but we've got absolutely nothing in common, no idea of civilized debate.

'Look, Eddie.' Dee goes back to her handbag, fishing out a small hanky and passing it in his direction without looking at him. 'There. Actually,' she stands with her back to him and the room sounds with his sobbing, 'I wasn't going to tell you this. I was going to save it but I might as well. The point is that really we have nothing to fear. There is no lime-pit, Eddie, and the rumour about gassing was just . . .'

Eddie's books stacked, ready to go on the table, Eddie's globe. Dee turns the globe, spinning it faster and faster; her hands are shaking now and the globe falls to the floor.

'It's all right, Eddie. Only a tiny dent. Nothing to worry about, nothing to fear. Earth's not flat now, is it?' Dee puts her hand in the dent she has made somewhere over an ocean she cannot read without her glasses on. 'Beautiful, beautiful dip,' she says. 'Little hollow, shallow dip. We only need a little dip, the two of us,' she muses, 'now that Sheila and William . . .

'Just because the radiators aren't on,' she continues in a stronger voice, 'isn't any reason for panic. If the worst comes to the worst then I've put it on paper. I wrote the whole thing up before I went to sleep last night. I've told them, categorically, that at our . . . that at this stage in our relationship, there is no question of splitting us up. Yes, I have had . . . well, you know only too well . . . Sheila, I mean . . . It's all right, Eddie, I can mention her by name. Water under the bridge, my dear. In the circumstances, compared to me, you've been circumspect. I wrote a list and

I put one of those massive brackets round it, you know the sort of thing they have on sheets of music. A list of my . . . dalliances. It took some nerve to do it but I did it, the whole thing with Derek Jacobi right up at the top. The only one I didn't mention was Hubert, (a) because it wasn't consummated and (b) because try as I might to avoid the facts it's obvious to me at least that he's probably long dead.

'What I've written is that there is no way that you and I will sanction being parted. There's no need to worry, Eddie, wherever we go it's together or not at all. It's horses for courses, Eddie, they can expect some very drastic action if there's even a shadow of a suggestion of any . . . nefarious . . . and actually, you know how odd it is . . . things come to you *in extremis*, don't you think?

'I said somewhere in the Netherlands might meet our criteria though we do need photographs and proof. I know some people think I'm somewhat scatty, but the truth is that I never miss a trick. I listen, Eddie, and when I listen, believe me, I take things in. I had a long talk with Hubert about the Netherlands, it must have been, oh, I don't know, eight, ten years ago? They had *en suite* bathrooms as far back as at least 1964. It'll surprise Orchid but then she needs a jolt. I put it in writing, "Don't worry your head about the car," I said, "We're perfectly amenable to aeroplane or boat."'

If nothing is any earthly good then anything is something . . . It was when the heating was turned off for good, when the twanging of contracting radiators sounded for the last time, that Eddie decided that he must do something, that he must act now before it was too late. Clearing the contents of his small bedside locker he steeled himself to look again at William's drawings, to reread William's notes.

Blunt gloves, ruffs fringed with jet, purple drapes swagged across the railings of the Wet Weather Room, interspersed with skulls, crossed bones and sand timers, instructions in the minutest detail – William had thought of everything apart from the possibility of his own death. He had drawn it all, all the trappings of *pompes funèbres;* an elaborate send-off was what he had had in mind. An orgy of mourning, not simply for Sheila but for all the known and unknown dead who beg to be remembered, the dead in the graves in the sloping cemetery beyond the arms of the bird-messed alabaster angel. Bombazine and crape for them, black ostrich feathers for them, William had drawn it and given it to Eddie for safekeeping.

The substance and shape of the soul that Eddie did not believe in had been painstakingly drawn and described: ovals to be released by inmates dressed in funereal black, ovals borne up in the thermals of the four corners of the Airing Court, 'Ovals light enough to float like blossom.' And Eddie recalled the metalworker's mask that William had shown him during the slide show ... Eddie had been the rock that William sheltered under, the only thing safer than Eddie was death and Eddie's impulse was to throw the evidence away. His head said destroy it all, but his heart stayed his fingers, his conscience pricked him and the irony of whether he had left it too late to redeem himself by carrying out William's instructions proved ultimately too much to bear.

No Ridout, no Verne, but Fatty Barrett had said that he was up for anything and Ruck too was in favour. Mentioning anything to Dee would be a death wish, but Maisie was reliable, she could sew, and there were one or two others ...

Souls to be cut from the gauze of metalworkers' masks. 'Must be white, immaculate,' William had written. 'Ask Ridout for gloves.' But Ridout could not hear him now. 'Bombazine or crape.' Too late for anything like that now but Eddie remembered the black cloth for the slide show; it was easy to tear it into the simplest shape that would cover them, with a rough hole for their heads . . .

On Hilversum, Luxembourg and Roma they are sewing in the night. Dishevelled, puffy-eyed, dressed in an assortment of washed-out blue-and-white-striped issue pyjamas, coats and jumpers, convulsive hands tack along the thick chalk lines following the arrows, themselves undulating, drawn in by Maisie the Pattern Maker. Lips are pursed, eyes screwed and bedside lights tilted to illuminate the piece they are tiredly sewing. Shaking hands and fluttering fingers, the twitch, the tick and the tremor that goes with the territory of drugs; the sudden jerk that sends the black material slipping off the bed and down on to the lino; the stitch too long and wide of the mark. Concentration is the hard thing, comfort is the hard thing, the hardest thing is keeping fingers warm enough to work. Backstitch, backstitch and oversew. Fatty Barrett pins shoulders and sides together; Ruck dozes off while he is waiting for the next one. Fingers that will not comply with the necessary stitching rhythm, brains that wander idly as they sew, off along the passageways and corridors, feeling for the latch and then the light switch, down alleys into the culs-de-sac that have stalled them so many times before.

Concentration is the hard thing, comfort is the hard thing. Ruck has propped himself up by lumping all his bedclothes behind his back. He has a coat over his legs and two pairs of socks on. Although cold, Fatty Barrett has the ventilator open to keep himself awake. At quarter to two in the morning there is nothing but the sodium hiss that makes the orange glare outside. Eddie sits at the top of the dormitory cross-legged, shoulders taut with concentration. He uses an oval of metal as a template, two souls cut out of every mask with a little pair of nail scissors and two hot and gleaming red welts around the thumb and forefinger of his right hand. Twice already he has been up and around, chivvying the others, reminding those who have forgotten that though the ritual of mourning may not be practised outside these walls, they do things properly in here. Round and round he cuts with the scissors, punishing his hands. What surprised him most was how easy it had been to galvanize their interest.

'The soul goes marching on,' says Fatty Barrett, who claims a voice like an angel and says they all should sing 'John Brown's Body' at the moment of release. And Ruck suggests that the night to do it is the longest night of the shortest day.

The shape and the colour of the soul goes undisputed, although no one had ever seen a soul (although if there is a god he has long ago abandoned them). So Eddie cuts the ovals, but as he cuts the small residue of belief he has begins to falter. William's image of white discs thrown by black-garbed men begins to deconstruct, though Eddie would like to believe in it – is trying to believe in it, is working in the half-light with his heart and not his head. No seaside tiredness, this, but true exhaustion; white discs released by black-garbed men float beyond the reach of his imagination, replaced in PAIN by souls the size of the cracked side plates stacked in Doreen Brande's canteen. Side-plate souls, crazed by dish washing, rolling downhill away from him only to be checked by the tufts of grass that poke up through the asphalt of the Airing Court, sunk in the puddles on the tarmac, caught in the gratings of the drains. He peers into the half-light after them; how to tell in the murk of the forest, in the darkness that surrounds him, if they ever come to rest?